FORWARD MISSION

EDITED UNDER THE DIRECTION OF
YOUNG PEOPLE'S MISSIONARY MOVEMENT

THE FRONTIER

WARD PLATT

NEW YORK
YOUNG PEOPLE'S MISSIONARY MOVEMENT
OF THE UNITED STATES AND CANADA
1908

COPYRIGHT, 1908, BY
YOUNG PEOPLE'S MISSIONARY MOVEMENT
OF THE UNITED STATES AND CANADA

COMING OF THE WHITE MAN, STATUE, CITY PARK, PORTLAND, OREGON

TO
MY HELPMEET
WHO WALKED WITH GOD—AND WAS NOT
SHE LOVED THE MASTER'S MISSIONARY CALL
A KINDRED SPIRIT
MY OTHER SELF
MARY

CONTENTS

CHAPTER		PAGE
	Preface	xi
I	The Frontier—In the Making	1
II	Transforming the Desert	39
III	The Giant Northwest	75
IV	The West Between and Beyond	115
V	The New Southwest	151
VI	The American Indians and Some Other Peoples	181
VII	The West and the East	221

APPENDIXES

A	Table Showing Original Territory and Additions to the United States in Area and Population	255
B	Land Area, Population, and Density of Population for 1900 and 1906, by States and Territories	256
C	Vacant and Reserved Areas in the Western Public Land States	257
D	Irrigation Projects	258
E	Text of the Present Irrigation Law	259
F	Bibliography	265
	Index	281

ILLUSTRATIONS

	PAGE
Coming of the White Man, Statue, City Park, Portland, Oregon............Frontispiece	
Lower Yellowstone Project, Montana............	9
One of the Many Houses of Settlers Near Rupert, Idaho	9
Physical Map of the United States..............	43
Raising Grapes in the Salt River Valley, Near Mesa, Arizona............................	47
Date Tree in Salt River Valley, Near Mesa, Arizona	47
Building Homes in Anticipation of the Opening of Government Works, Arizona............	57
Home Near Phœnix, Arizona, Showing What Irrigation Will Do for the Desert...............	57
Second Avenue and Cherry Street, Seattle, Washington	79
Lumber Camp, Rainier, Oregon.................	93
The Richest Hill on Earth, Butte, Montana......	93
The Pride of the Mormons—the Temple, Salt Lake City, Utah...................................	131
Truckee-Carson Project, Nevada...............	141
Pure-blooded Apache Laborers Constructing a Road Through the Desert...................	141
Main Street of an Oklahoma Town, August Sixth.	165
Main Street of Same Town, August Sixteenth....	165
Main Street of Same Town, November Sixth, Same Year...................................	165

x   Illustrations

	PAGE
Blanket Indian Evangelistic Convention of Oklahoma	201
Anglo-Japanese Training School, San Francisco, California	209
Japanese Buddhist Mission and Pastor, San Francisco, California	209
Chinese Pastor and Family, Portland, Oregon	215
Choir of the Chinese Church, San Francisco, California	215
Plymouth Congregational Church, Seattle, Washington	229
Mexican Home Mission Baptist Church, El Paso, Texas	229
Baptist White Temple, Oklahoma City, Oklahoma	247
Map of the United States, Showing Territorial Growth	End

A FIRST WORD

The last five years have given us a new frontier. This book attempts to scan its outline and mark a few of its home missionary opportunities. The task is fragmentary and incomplete, as sources of information are meager. That conditions are unprecedented and the missionary situation critical is evident.

While blazing the way, we have endeavored to point out strategic positions and call attention to certain centers where multitudes are gathering for a momentous world movement.

The Church will doubtless meet this situation by volunteer brigades and forced marches.

A reader of *American History and Its Geographic Conditions,* by Ellen Churchill Semple, and *The History of the Pacific Northwest,* by Joseph Schafer, also *The Conquest of Arid America,* by William E. Smythe will readily note my indebtedness in chapters one and two to these books.

Much other information, because recent, has been gathered from so wide a range of periodicals as to make impracticable a specific acknowledgment.

The Secretaries of the various Home Boards have coöperated. The Editorial Committee of the Young People's Missionary Movement has contributed valuable suggestions, and Dr. A. J. Kynett of Philadelphia has made available helpful literature.

WARD PLATT.

Philadelphia, Pa., August 25, 1908.

THE FRONTIER—IN THE MAKING

At first the frontier was the Atlantic coast. It was the frontier of Europe in a very real sense. Moving westward, the frontier became more and more American. As successive terminal moraines result from successive glaciations, so each frontier leaves its traces behind it, and when it becomes a settled area the region still partakes of the frontier characteristics. Thus the advance of the frontier has meant a steady movement away from the influence of Europe, a steady growth of independence on American lines. And to study this advance, the men who grew up under these conditions, and the political, economic, and social results of it, is to study the really American part of our history.

—*Turner*

The world's scepter passed from Persia to Greece, from Greece to Italy, from Italy to Great Britain, and from Great Britain the scepter is to-day departing. It is passing on to "Greater Britain," to our mighty West, there to remain, for there is no farther West; beyond is the Orient. Like the star in the East which guided the three kings with their treasures westward until at length it stood still over the cradle of the young Christ, so the star of empire, rising in the East, has ever beckoned the wealth and power of the nations westward, until to-day it stands still over the cradle of the young empire of the West, to which the nations are bringing their offerings.

The West is to-day an infant, but shall one day be a giant in each of whose limbs shall unite the strength of many nations.

—*Strong*

I

THE FRONTIER—IN THE MAKING

World navigation and world history may be divided into three stages: the Mediterranean which stands for past history, the Atlantic which means the present, and the Pacific which holds the future. History was shifted from the Mediterranean to the Atlantic in an attempt to find an ocean route to the Orient.

Three Stages of World History

Fundamental to the history of the United States is its location on the Atlantic opposite Europe, and a significant fact connected with its future is its location on the Pacific opposite Asia.[1] Our geographical position places us in the center of things both in relation to Europe and the Orient. Our location is in the temperate zone and from ocean to ocean. Our climate gives us an energetic population. Geographically and providentially we control the western hemisphere. This, coupled with the

Central Position of the United States

---

[1] Semple, *American History and Its Geographic Conditions*, 91. This work has also suggested several of the views of the bearing of geography upon our early development indicated in the ten or eleven pages which follow.

3

fact that the United States was peopled by an Anglo-Saxon race, determined our destiny.

Our Western Expansion

Our area of three millions of square miles is twice as great from east to west as from north to south. This means a westward expansion. Down our central valley not only sweep the cold winds from the north, but up it also blow the gentle breezes of the Gulf. The northern Rockies, low and more narrow than farther south, permit the passage of the Pacific winds which bring warmth and moisture to Montana and the Dakotas.

World Comparisons

The position of the United States over against that of China is strategic, because China presents a future of possible productiveness on a large scale, more similar to that of the United States than any other country of the globe. But China suffers because she has not profited by her location and because of a lack of navigable rivers. Russia is not a formidable competitor of the United States because of her subarctic situation. Japan makes remarkable progress but lacks area and population. English Pacific possessions are too far away from the center of power, which lies between the thirtieth and fortieth parallels of north latitude.

In the Making

Significance of the Pacific

In the light of modern history we are able to appreciate the immense importance of our every accession of territory bordering on the Pacific. Hawaii in its location is providential. Our trade with the Orient steadily increases. We are sure to dominate the Pacific and to exert over the Orient a correspondingly great influence. The importance of the development of the West as a basis of this new world influence is apparent.

How Explorations Were Directed

Search for Northwest Passage

The most desirable section of the temperate zone in North America is between the twenty-fifth and fiftieth degrees north latitude. In this belt are located our chief Atlantic streams. Providence led European navigators, by their search for a northwest passage, to know much about that portion of our country essential to the development of the United States, and later of the world at large. This search of the explorers resulted, not in the discovery of a passage, but of an immense supply of peltries; and thus the passion of the navigators was shifted, as one has said, from passage to peltries.

Effect of Fur Trade

This trade resulted in a most thorough exploration of our shores, rivers, and streams.

Thus, in early days, the fur-bearing animals enticed men into intimate knowledge of our country east of the Mississippi. The fur supply from the earlier discovered streams became exhausted and made it necessary to push on and discover other waters.

North American Basins

A mighty trough runs through the middle of our continent from the Arctic Ocean to the Gulf of Mexico. About midway it is met by an eastward valley in which are the Great Lakes. The rim separating these two valleys is low and narrow and is near to the lakes. The earlier explorers were obliged to carry their canoes on this rim from but one to ten miles to launch again on waters that run into the Mississippi River. This geographical fact greatly stimulated early explorations.

Natural Features

Appalachian Mountains an Early Factor

The Appalachian Mountains have had an important influence on our history. This range of mountains so compassed the original thirteen colonies that it welded them into a national life. This made the American Revolution possible, and under God successful. But for these mountain barriers, apart from dangers from Indians, the colonists might have spread out so thinly as to have resulted in a national consciousness so attenuated as to have made resistance to Great Britain improbable. And yet while this system of mountains offered for the time being a convenient barrier to secure for us this very important chapter of our history, the average elevation of these ranges is only three or four thousand feet. This, in the fulness of time, did not stand in the way of an overflow westward.

The only important gateway was through the Mohawk and Hudson valleys. This pass was only about four hundred and forty-five feet above sea-level. Easy trails led from the Mohawk and the Genesee to the upper Allegheny and thence to the Ohio and Mississippi. The Hudson and Mohawk valleys held the key to the early northwest even as the meeting of the Allegheny and Monongahela commanded the "gateway of the West." *One Important Gateway*

Western Pioneer Advance

The people who early pushed westward and those who came to settle in the whole stretch of the Appalachian Mountains formed a backwoods democracy in contrast to the aristocratic inhabitants of the plantation. Large farms *Mountain or Backwoods Democracy* were not possible in the mountain regions and the necessities common to these isolated communities placed all on a common level and engendered a resourceful and self-reliant spirit. Thus was a people developed for the conquest of the larger West.

Overflow Westward

In course of time these Appalachian settlements overflowed into Tennessee and Kentucky, covered great stretches of the Ohio River country, and onward to the Mississippi. Here was developed a new type of Americans, "the sturdy, youthful American of the western wilds." They became so separated by natural barriers from the Atlantic coast states as to make necessary something of a compacted life for defense against the Indians, and for the promotion of common interests inherent in those early infant commonwealths.

English Pioneers Permanent Occupants

The English pioneer, however, was distinct from the French trader by his sedentary occupation of the land. This meant permanent occupancy, and foretold the future of the country as a whole. These more western communities came gradually to such a robust and self-reliant development as to finally result in pushing our national boundary line across the Mississippi into Texas; and really forced our

LOWER YELLOWSTONE PROJECT, MONTANA
ONE OF THE MANY HOUSES OF SETTLERS NEAR RUPERT, IDAHO

government, in the years following, into the extension of its domain, step by step, to the Pacific.

These western and other advancing settlers kept Congress in a state of chronic anxiety. Had not the United States secured from Napoleon the Louisiana Purchase, our own people who had even then crossed the Mississippi in great numbers might have formed a government for themselves. In fact the East was somewhat apprehensive concerning the westward tide for fear a new commonwealth might be formed and detach itself from the original government. Even as late as the building of the first transcontinental railroad, Congress was influenced by the probability that unless extensive land grants were made the builders of the road to insure a connection between the Pacific coast and the East, that whole rich western section might establish its own government. *Interest of Congress*

Results of the Louisiana Purchase

Up to the time of the Louisiana Purchase we had been governed largely by the ocean. The colonies clustering along the Atlantic were dominated by it. This continued until the Republic was forty years old. Intercolonial com- *Continental Expansion Followed Louisiana Purchase* munication was by sea. Thus we were a seafaring people occupying the most advantageous coast on the American continent, but now, with our immense extension westward, there began in 1830 a widespread movement of population in that direction as far as to the 95th meridian. It lingered there for many years. Our development became continental as opposed to maritime. Our merchant marine began to decline, and ever since we have been preeminently a nation of the soil. Our expansion westward began to be blocked out from 1810 to 1820, and that portion of our advance was not completed until 1840.

Advance Along Rivers

For twenty-five years after the war of 1812 there was a large movement of our population to the Mississippi Valley, which was augmented by a tide of immigration that set in from Europe at the close of the Napoleonic wars. Steam navigation on lake and river was then so well established as to facilitate this movement. If one were to consult a map indicating the advance of population at that time, he might note bulges westward; these bulges were in most cases along the courses of rivers. In 1820 these protrusions began to look like long fingers. Between these were many vacant spots; but these were rough mountain ranges, swamps, relatively barren country, or large tracts held by Indian tribes. Between 1830 and 1840 these Indian lands were gradually occupied and the tribes removed to the Indian Territory.

Historic Trails

By 1840 we had a narrow frontier zone approaching the 95th meridian and the northern boundary of the Missouri River. The advance paused here, as this was the margin of the arid belt and the eastern boundary of the Indian Territory. But beyond this was a frontier of arid land, snowy mountains, and dread desert stretching away to the Pacific. Venturesome souls were constantly pushing out and across this mysterious region. Only one river in that wide expanse, the Missouri, has sufficient flow of water to become a considerable avenue of travel. Thus this river determined the larger immigration to the Northwest. Lewis and Clark followed this course. At Independence the Missouri makes a bend northwest. This necessitated the beginning of the prairie trails westward. In the valley of the Upper Rio Grande there is a natural gateway through the mountain barrier of the Rockies. This ac-

The Missouri and Westward Trails

counts for the old city of Santa Fé, and that early route from Independence to Santa Fé was known as the Santa Fé Trail.

California Trails

Santa Fé, because of its geographical location, became the center of expansion to the Pacific. The natural advance was by the route of Kit Carson's famous ride in 1840, the Gila Trail ending at San Diego, southern California, which country was soon brought into intercourse with the United States. A more northern route called the Spanish Trail led to Los Angeles. Our restless population was also turning to Oregon, a name covering the great Northwest.

Oregon Trail

By 1840 the Oregon Trail started like the Santa Fé Trail, from Independence, Missouri. It traversed a distance of twenty-four hundred miles and became a much traveled route. One reason for this was that the soil of Missouri was very productive and this inland country afforded no outlet for a market. So congested became the Missouri market that a farmer sold "a boat load of bacon and lard for a hundred dollars and the Mississippi steamboats at times found in bacon a hot and cheap fuel." Access to the sea became a necessity. This meant greatly augmented emigration to Oregon. The sufferings by these caravans crossing the desert are difficult for us to comprehend, and yet these intrepid frontier people pressed on by hundreds and thousands. The qualities born of their hardships were not among the least of their desert cargoes.

By 1853 the Gadsden Purchase from Mexico extended our southwest border from the Gila River to the southern watershed. In this addition ten millions of dollars were paid for forty-five thousand acres of land almost entirely unfit for occupation. But it was money well expended as it gave us a passageway to the Pacific always open, along a low level, and never blocked by snow. Our vast territory coupled with our isolation from Europe incited to an early dream of continental power. Out of this grew the Monroe Doctrine.

Gadsden Purchase— Monroe Doctrine

Pacific Discovery

The story of the western frontier begins first with explorations of the Pacific coast. This was started by the Spaniards in 1513, was continued by various voyagers for a period of two hundred and sixty-five years, and closed with Captain Cook in his discovery of Cape Prince of Wales.

Genesis of the Western Frontier

Balboa's Discovery

It was in 1513 that Balboa first beheld the Pacific, and declared that by right of discovery all its coast belonged to the King of Spain. "Since the time of Columbus, Spain had been searching among the West Indies and along the Atlantic coast of Central and South America in the hope of finding an open passage to the Orient."

The Spanish Search for Passage

The Spaniards, from a commercial standpoint, were in great need of this looked-for strait, and a search for the same began along the Pacific coast. In 1523 Lake Nicaragua was discovered and the Panama Canal project suggested itself to the Spaniards.

Effect of Destruction of Armada

In 1588 the English destroyed the Spanish Armada. Spain was thus no longer feared, and England, France, and Holland began to colonize the new world.

Spain and Great Britain as Rivals on the Pacific

Spain was now fearful that Great Britain might be successful in her search for a northwest passage and drive her off the Pacific; hence the people of Mexico, helped by the Spanish Government, made unusual exertions for the safety of Spain. This involved an extensive plan for expansion northward. They were to colonize, build forts, and bring the entire region of upper California under Spanish rule. They planned to possess the shores of the north Pacific. In addition was the project of planting missions for Christianizing the Indians. The first mission was founded at San Diego in 1769. The romantic ruins of these missions still remain in California. In 1776 England sent its great discoverer, Captain Cook, to the Pacific to make further search for a northwest passage. Although Cook never returned to England, what seemed incidental to his voyage was attended with momentous results.

As he pursued his way along the northwest coast, the Indians from time to time came to the ship to exchange sea-otter and other skins for trinkets from the white man. The sailors themselves did not know the value of these skins, but on their return home the ship touched at Canton, China, and the unused furs, which had cost the sailors not a sixpence sterling each, brought as much as a hundred dollars apiece. The crew was wild to return for another cargo. This was not permitted. But instantly the attention of the world was turned to the northwest coast. In a few years men of every nation were among the mariners who cruised along that shore to trade with the Indians.

Value of the Fur Trade Discovered

American Ship Enters the Columbia River

Several Boston merchants in 1787 fitted out two small vessels, the *Columbia* and *Lady Washington,* with cargoes of articles both cheap and attractive to the Indians. The *Columbia* was commanded by Captain Gray. One purchase was that of two hundred otter skins for a chisel. Gray after disposing of his cargo of skins in China returned to Boston with a ship-load of tea by way of the Cape of Good Hope, and thus was the first sailor under the American flag to circumnavigate the globe. Later, in 1791, in the *Columbia,* he returned to the Pacific Coast, and on May 11, 1792, entered the mouth of a river, latitude 46° 10′, and named it Columbia River in honor of his good ship the *Columbia.*

Importance of the Discovery

Thus this incident of the fur trade resulted in the discovery, by a representative of the United States, of the Columbia River, up which he sailed some thirty miles. Seventeen years before this Spaniards had discovered the bay at the mouth of the river and suspected its existence but failed to enter it.

English Opportunities Lost

Four years before Gray's discovery of the river an English trader noted the indentations made by the river's mouth, and called it Deception Bay, and declared no river was there

In the Making

as laid down on the Spanish charts. In 1778 Captain Cook had passed up the coast without knowing the presence of the river, and only two weeks before Gray made his discovery Captain Vancouver examined the opening but thought it a small inlet or river not accessible to "vessels of our burden." Thus by a very narrow margin was the Columbia River and the northwest province saved to the United States.

The Louisiana Purchase

The country west of the Mississippi River was supposed to be in the possession of Spain. The fact was, however, that Napoleon in 1800 had forced Spain to give back to France this territory called Louisiana, a name covering most of the country west of the Mississippi to the Rocky Mountains. *"Louisiana" a French Acquisition*

When a little later the Americans learned of this change of ownership, great uneasiness was felt among the western settlers. There was at this time probably a total of 325,000 white people whose prospects were in the hands of the power that controlled the Mississippi River. All their salable produce must find a market in New Orleans, down this river, and if an alien power interfered with the free navigation of *Jefferson Secures This Territory for the United States* these waters it meant untold hardship to them. They did not fear Spain, who owned the land on both sides of the river, but the French nation was far more powerful. War with France was talked of. Jefferson, however, by able diplomacy purchased "Louisiana" from Napoleon, and this immense stretch westward doubled the area of the United States.

Lewis and Clark Expedition

Even before this was effected, Jefferson had arranged with Lewis, his private secretary, and with Clark, an able associate, to explore the country to the Pacific Ocean. His plea to Congress for an appropriation was most unique. He suggested possible friendly relations with the Indian tribes which, among other things, might result in a sale of plows to the savages. This would encourage them in agriculture and result in less land for their hunting-grounds. In his desire for a larger knowledge of the West, he was, in his dealings with Congress, to say the least, a tactful man. An appropriation of twenty-five hundred dollars was secured for the expedition. Thus Lewis and Clark, whose annals and whose travels have been much talked of, followed the Missouri River from St. Louis and explored portions of the Northwest as far as the Pacific Ocean. This expedition, together with Gray's discovery of the Columbia, gave the United States a good claim upon the Oregon country, which was not included in the Louisiana Purchase.

Saving the Pacific Northwest

But the only way the United States could establish its claim to the Pacific Northwest to the forty-ninth degree was to colonize the country. The various ventures in fur trading had resulted in a small occupancy. The first efforts toward settlement began in 1831 or 1832, when a Nez Percés delegation of four Indians came to St. Louis to inquire about "The white man's God in heaven." They came in search of General Clark whom they had met when he was west on the Lewis and Clark expedition. Clark, being a Catholic, did not tell them about the Bible. The whole story of this strange embassy, only one of whom returned to his people with his sad story, got abroad in the newspapers and found a hearty response among New Englanders. *Factors Leading to Colonization*

In 1833 the Methodist denomination sent out the Rev. Jason Lee and other colaborers as missionaries to the Indians. He began work on the Willamette River. The missionaries found *Missionary Movement Under Jason Lee* there about twelve white men having farms along the river. They had married Indian wives. Most of them were servants of the Hudson's Bay Company. This was the beginning of the first agricultural colony in Oregon. The missionaries were more successful among whites than Indians. They opened a school, started religious services, and even organized a temperance society which a number of the white men joined.

Further Progress

Work was continued among the Indians and gratifying progress was made among the children some of whom attended the school. In 1837 the missionaries were reenforced by twenty assistants. The Indian work, however, did not flourish, as the natives were a degraded race and were dying off at a rapid rate.

Marcus Whitman

Two years after the departure of Lee for Oregon the American Board sent out a young physician, Dr. Marcus Whitman, and others. Whitman began work two hundred and fifty miles inland, on the Walla Walla River. The white settlements slowly grew. In the fall of 1837 six hundred head of stock were brought up from California.

Government Agent's Report

The government sent out an agent to inspect the settlement. His report to Congress aroused great interest. He insisted that the United States must never accept a northern boundary that would give Puget Sound to Canada. It must hold out for the forty-ninth degree of north latitude.

The formative centers and the sources of organizing and fostering influences for these early colonists were really the missions established by Jason Lee and Marcus Whitman. *Formative Centers*

Lee, returning to the United States in 1838 to obtain reenforcements, was accompanied by two Indian boys. This awakened enthusiasm. Petitions and memorials emanated from these missions to Congress calling attention to the advantages of the country and asking for protection as subjects of the United States. Lee and Whitman were very prominent in these matters. Each visited Washington, where he talked with the President and others concerning the future of Oregon. Lee received forty-two thousand dollars as the result of his trip to the east for reenforcements to the work. He took back with him to Oregon a company of more than fifty persons—men, women, and children. This with the trappers who settled in that region about that time constituted a colony of more than a hundred people. Whit- *Visits to the East and Reenforcements* man also conducted a large company from the East. In 1834 more than one thousand persons were organized into a caravan and made the journey safely. The next year fourteen hundred crossed the desert, and in the year after, three thousand. This last reenforcement doubled the white population of Oregon, which now numbered about six thousand. They settled in five communities.

Provisional Government

As the United States provided no government for this territory, delaying to do so because the inhabitants were determined that it should not be a pro-slavery state, the people themselves created a provisional government, which continued for some time after the Oregon boundary question was settled between the United States and Great Britain in 1846.

Influence of Heroic Lives

About this time occurred Marcus Whitman's remarkable ride to the East and later still, in November, 1847, the massacre of himself and others by the Indians. The influence of the mission stations of Jason Lee and Marcus Whitman upon these early settlements and provisional governments, also the character of the people brought into the Northwest thereby, molded the future firm Christian sentiment of our Northwest. They are elemental forces to be recognized by the historian. The narrative of the labors of Whitman and Lee and their worthy helpers is an inspiring story. It abounds in highest examples of the heroic. These annals must be read in order to appreciate the potential and self-sacrificing services rendered by these early statesmen in the interests of the broadest patriotism and the kingdom of Jesus Christ.

California

A New Center of Settlement

While Oregon was developing as described in the preceding narrative, California was attracting attention. This part of the country was under the Spanish rule of Mexico. In 1841 the first company of immigrants arrived in the Sacramento Valley. They went partly by the Oregon trail, and, for a time after this, the annual caravan westward divided at Fort Hall, the larger number going to Oregon, but a part to California.

Sacramento Valley

Captain John Sutter in 1839 secured from the Mexican government eleven square leagues of land in the Sacramento Valley. He built an adobe home, began to farm and raise cattle on a large scale, and carried on a fur trade with the Indians. This was on the main immigrant route from the United States to Oregon. The Mexican government was so weak at this time that the Americans did much as they chose until some four or five thousand were scattered throughout the valley and over the plains of California. They were mostly cattle herders and traded with American ships from New England.

Cession of Territory to the United States

Misunderstandings with the Mexican government and continued immigration to California at last culminated in the raising of the "Lone Star" flag, which heralded the declaration of California's independence from Mexico. After the war, in which General John C. Fremont, the "Pathfinder," took part, and which lasted about a year and a half, the territory was ceded to the United States.

Effect of the Discovery of Gold

Ten days before the signing of the treaty, an event occurred most momentous to the West. Some fifty miles above Sutter's Fort, on January 24, 1848, James W. Marshall made his world-famous discovery of gold. All at Sutter's wished to keep the discovery a secret, but it escaped. In a few weeks there was a great inrush of inhabitants armed with shovels and pans. In San Francisco and other towns, ordinary lines of business were suspended.

Business houses were deserted. Ships remained in San Francisco because they were abandoned by their crews. Picks, shovels, and pans rose to extraordinary prices. Within a year Oregon lost a large proportion of her men. The news went like wild-fire through the East. During the next spring twenty-five thousand persons in caravans moved westward to Sacramento. This continued month after month and year after year. San Francisco became the commercial emporium of the West. Two years after the discovery of gold California had a population, mostly American, of ninety-two thousand, while Oregon, including all the territory west of the Rockies and north of California, had less than fourteen thousand people. By 1870 California's population had increased to five hundred and sixty thousand, while the Oregon territory had but one hundred and thirty thousand.

The early missionary exploits of Bishop William Taylor, the Rev. O. C. Wheeler, and other California pioneers belong to this part of the narrative. "The Argonauts of forty-nine" changed the Oregon trail to the California trail, and the emphasis for those years was changed from Oregon to California.

Bishop William Taylor, Rev. O. C. Wheeler, and Others

Railways to the Pacific

In May, 1869, fifty miles west of Ogden, Utah, was driven the golden spike which united the Union Pacific and the Central Pacific Railways. From this time on other transcontinental railways, both north and south, were constructed. Minor roads in the Northwest were completed. The effect on western states and the country generally was most marked. This is seen in the fact that while in the Northwest there was in 1870 a total of one hundred and thirty thousand inhabitants, in ten years thereafter there were added one hundred and fifty-two thousand five hundred, and in the next ten years four hundred and sixty-five thousand.

Wonderful Growth of California and the Northwest

California in its cities and agricultural wealth has become a garden of the world. It is so advanced toward what makes up an ideal commonwealth that it can in part only be classed a frontier. Since 1870 the gain in the Northwest has been considerably more rapid than that of California. The growth of a number of these states is like a dream and would seem incredible were not the facts beyond question.[1]

---

[1] For a further study of dates and facts concerning Pacific discovery and its results, see Schafer, *History of the Pacific Northwest*, to which our indebtedness is acknowledged

Our Debt to the Pioneer

We shall never give proper credit to the intrepid pioneers of the frontier. We are not able to do so because we cannot realize what they endured. Their journeys, whether by sea in the primitive craft of those rude times, or by land through trackless forests where shelter other than nature provided was impossible, where wild beasts and savages tracked these scouts of our dawning civilization—these journeys alone are beyond the power of this generation to understand, for we have nothing in our own experience or within our range of observation by which to make comparisons.

What the Early Pioneers Endured

Still further removed from our realm of knowledge are their journeys by river. The canoe is an unstable craft. One should be well trained and an expert swimmer to handle a canoe under conditions of his own choosing. But more perilous would it be to load one with the few belongings making up one's store of necessities, to do this in a wilderness isolation where even money cannot reproduce them, to put into another a wife and little one, and then to commit all to uncertain currents and perilous rapids, and to glide on, a helpless mark for the

Perils of Rivers

lurking wildman's arrow or rifle. And most venturesome was the attempt to voyage up stream, a strenuous advance against current and tempest with progress painfully slow. The journey may of necessity be in winter when men battle with forming ice and camp at night in deep snow, their fires kept low and inadequate lest the light make them targets for inhuman foes.

Merciless Rapids

Rapids were successfully shot only by a skill foreign to any training known to us. Such aptness was part of the secrets wrested from the great wild of nature by persistent and ceaseless struggle with her untamed forces. Sometimes all that stood between life endurable and extreme privation, the meager supplies of one or more families, went to the bottom. Or again in the raging rapids a frail bark overturned and wife, mother and tender little child were whirled helplessly down among rocks and merciless waters.

Experiences Too Deep for Words

Words die in silence. The pioneer goes on alone like some stricken prophet, freighted with a message to be passed on to a people whom he knows not and who can never know him, much less can they feel his heart-throbs which become the pulse-beats of a nation's life.

If progress were across a desert, then sufferings still more intense pursue him. His schooner of the waste is piloted along a track marked at intervals by bones where animals perished with thirst. The pitiless, monotonous expanse, sagebrush and alkali, a sea of land stretching to the shimmering horizon, a horizon that recedes with the journey and, after weeks of slow advance, seems still as far away. Water may be had only at intervals of miles, and the brackish, meager supply is found by the practised vision of experience. By day heat, sand-storms that defy language, and reptiles loathsome and venomous. At night a cold drops out of the immensity and he shiveringly scans a vault above him so black that the stars are of unwonted size and burn with an intensity that seems born of the glare of the day. About him the measureless wastes lie in somber shadows, and the oppressive stillness is relieved only by the howl and cry of wild creatures whose notes are keyed to the awful wilderness that shelters them.

Sufferings on the Desert

To cross the desert in a Pullman car upholstered and stocked with delicacies is to invade a region where desolation hangs in the very air and discomfort pierces plate glass barriers two

Dreariness Beyond Expression

windows thick. The absolute dreariness of the arid wastes of our West are beyond expression. They record themselves in human consciousness but cannot be reproduced in speech.

Favored Visitors of the Desert

Certain souls, who live on the desert margin and feel its lure, break at intervals through its barriers and venture a few days' journey, warily undertaken, and with all due precaution. Such may see beauty by day and discourse entertainingly on rattlers, and side-winders, and lizards, and the weird scenery of desert growth and color. At night the sky to them pulsates with poetry and a wild charm enthralls them. They talk of the freedom of elemental life; but this is all recreation on the fringe of a monster wilderness. Their brief holiday trip and its temporary privations will, on their return, give zest and flavor to an otherwise jaded life. Even under such circumstances the desert at best is awful.

Intrepid Layers of Foundations

Our forefather pioneers were bent on no holiday. With their little all they played not on the borders of the pitiless American waste. They sternly invaded it. They faced its scorching heat, they bent before its blasts, and patiently braved its silences. They pushed grimly on, and slimly equipped and scantily provisioned endured it at its worst. They faced it for months and for more than two thousand miles. Those who lived, and most did, came out of it tried in endurance and affliction that made them ever after immune to the hardships of the wilds they came to conquer. God prepared Israel in Egypt and God as truly prepared our American forefathers for a conquest of this continent. Not to familiarize ourselves with the manner of their life, their privations, their hardships, the enforced alertness, and the nervous tension that made their existence possible, is to shut ourselves from what made us. It is to deprive ourselves of a fellowship of souls, a partial acquaintance with whom will broaden our sympathies, quicken our sensibilities, and enrich our lives with rare companionships. We are their successors. They laid foundations in blood and afflictions. Since then others have builded and at great cost. To us is transferred the task of carrying up walls partly finished, building far-reaching wings, and expressing in details of benevolence and beauty the meaning of the pioneer. Otherwise his life will have no adequate earthly expression, his privations will prove abortive, and our own lives will have little meaning.

Of Whom the World Was Not Worthy

Higher Missionary Motive

Other men and women, however, make up this picture of the past of our country. We say other, for they seem strangely set apart from other people. We mean the early missionaries who followed wherever the pioneer penetrated and where often the preacher proved the more intrepid. The pioneer for the most part was prompted by home hunger. The chance was his, even at a perilous venture, to carve out of stubborn possibilities a home. He knew that when once the journey was successfully made, and a few years of hard work had followed, a comfortable subsistence might be comparatively easy. And then the venture, the newness, the opposing elements, the distance, the mystery, "the call of the wild," all beckoned and allured those early Anglo-Saxons. It was in the blood.

Endurance Showing a Heaven-born Passion

But what of those souls who endured again and again all the privations of primitive travel and over and again compassed the same frontier; always homeless, always seeking those more needy than themselves; without adequate subsistence, enduring exposures, exertions, and discomforts unknown in older communities?

Going where they were not invited, often not wanted, they contended for the privilege of being benefactors. One could not hide from them nor move to a wilderness so remote that the missionary did not, as a matter of course, appear. His was a passion born of heaven.

Alert New England Enterprise

In God's far-reaching purpose he early stirred the people of New England, before a missionary society had been formed, and as early as 1793 nine pastors were set apart by their respective churches for a four months' absence. Four dollars and a half per week was allowed them for expenses and four dollars per week for pulpit supply. They followed early settlers into the frontiers of New York and elsewhere.

Remarkable Summary

In different ways Connecticut alone sent out, over a period of years, two hundred pastors who gave a total of five hundred years of service; and in a generation New England had spent, out of her penury following the long drain of the Revolutionary War, a quarter of a million dollars in sending the gospel to communities entirely outside her borders, save for a few Indians.[1]

Builders of Communities

Wherever early settlers went the missionary

---

[1] Clark, *Leavening the Nation*, 27–30.

followed. He was a formative factor. The annals of these men show what godless communities they invaded; how people who had once known better things had retrograded; how the Sabbath, in fact the entire decalogue, was virtually abrogated. Yet patiently, with a persistency more than human and with a wisdom and power direct from God, these men radiated influences and were the sources of currents that shaped communities and built up states. They could no more be resisted than the forces of nature.

Heralds of a Divine Message

Nature is an expression of God. His faithful servants are his organs of speech. Without the early preachers, frontiers would have lapsed to barbarism. Their evolution into orderly towns and law-observing commonwealths, their progress in intellectual and moral life, their stability and in short every element that to-day distinguishes them from utter paganism with all its poverty and hideousness, is as inseparable from the preacher as light from the sun. Whoever will know this may read for himself. He will be impressed no more with the surprising history than its abundant testimony concerning our debt to the pioneer preacher. He was God's herald trumpeting his proclamation, and as truly was his hand the instrument which molded our infant nation.

This statement concerning the influence of the preacher applies to our every national enlargement and to new phases of our history making for progress. Without him family relations relaxed, morality declined, progress stagnated, and civilization stranded. For example take a hundred years of southern mountain-white history.

The Home Missionary Indispensable

"So amid all sorts and conditions of men, and under a variety of circumstances, the minute-man lives, works, and dies, too often forgotten and unsung, but remembered in the Book; and when God shall make up his jewels, some of the brightest will be found among the pioneers who carried the ark into the wilderness in advance of the roads, breaking through the forest guided by the surveyor's blaze on the trees."[1]

Records of Sacrifice

The influences that shall emanate from our West and become a world-wide bane or blessing will be determined by our frontier home missionary investments: our fathers did their part. "They loved not their lives unto the

Successors of Heroes

---
[1] Puddefoot, *The Minute Man on the Frontier*, 44.

death." We are their successors. Their mantle falls on us. Shall we wear it or shift it?

QUESTIONS ON CHAPTER I

These questions have been prepared for the purpose of suggesting some new lines of thought that might not occur to the leader. They are not exhaustive, by any means, and every leader should study to use or replace according to his preference. Those marked * may afford an opportunity for discussion. Other questions demanding mere memory tests for reply can easily be added.

AIM: TO REALIZE THE PROVIDENTIAL DEVELOPMENT OF THE UNITED STATES AS A WORLD POWER

1. Name some of the early explorers of North America.
2. What were the explorers seeking when they discovered America?
3. Under what nations did they make their discoveries?
4. From what European countries did the first settlers come to America, and why?
5.* Name at least four admirable traits that were developed by the hardships endured by the early settlers of our country.
6.* What good effect did the Appalachian Mountains have on the development of the colonies?
7. Why did early expansion follow the great waterways?
8.* Name some of the results to the United States of the victory of Wolfe over Montcalm on the Heights of Abraham.

In the Making

9.* Sum up the results to the United States of the Revolution.
10. What section of the United States was occupied soon after the Revolution?
11. Why was Napoleon willing to sell the Louisiana Territory to the United States?
12. By how much was the territory of the United States increased by the acquisition of the Louisiana Territory?
13. How did the United States acquire Texas and Florida?
14. What were the circumstances that led to the acquisition of the Oregon Territory?
15. How did the United States obtain control of California and Mexico?
16.* What inventions in the early part of the nineteenth century made possible a more rapid development of the United States?
17. Name in the order of their importance the largest factors in the development of the United States.
18. Did the religious or commercial motives dominate in the development of our country?
19.* Do you believe that we could have attained our present position without the religious pioneers? Why not? Give several reasons.
20.* Name some of the advantages that our country has in its position between the two oceans.
21.* What physical advantages has the United States in location over Africa, South America, Russia, and China?
22. Compare the cultivable area of China with that of the United States.

23. What countries are competitors of the United States for the commercial supremacy of the world?
24. What advantages has the United States as a world power over Great Britain?
25. On what two countries does the present responsibility for world evangelization largely depend?

REFERENCES FOR FURTHER STUDY
CHAPTER I[1]

I. *Early Colonists.*
Clark: Leavening the Nation, II.
Gregg: Makers of the American Republic, I-VII.
Jenks: When America Was New, I-IV.
Prince: A Bird's-Eye View of American History, III-V, VII.
Strong: Our Country, XII.

II. *Louisiana Purchase.*
Carr: Missouri, IV, V.
Clark: Leavening the Nation, VII, X.
Hitchcock: Louisiana Purchase, VI-VIII.
Prince: A Bird's-Eye View of American History, 142-145.

III. *National Resources and Future of the United States.*
Strong: Our Country, II, XIV.

---
[1]Additional references will be found by consulting any good history of the United States, standard encyclopedia, and magazines.

TRANSFORMING THE DESERT

Irrigation is the foundation of truly scientific agriculture. Tilling the soil by dependence upon rainfall is, by comparison, like a stage-coach to the railroad, like the tallow dip to the electric light. The perfect conditions for scientific agriculture would be presented by a place where it never rained, but where a system of irrigation furnished a never-failing water-supply which could be adjusted to the varying needs of different plants. It is difficult for those who have been in the habit of thinking of irrigation as merely a substitute for rain to grasp the truth that precisely the contrary is the case. Rain is the poor dependence of those who cannot obtain the advantages of irrigation. The western farmer who has learned to irrigate thinks it would be quite as illogical for him to leave the watering of his potato patch to the caprice of the clouds as for the housewife to defer her wash-day until she could catch rainwater in her tubs.

The supreme advantage of irrigation consists not more in the fact that it assures moisture regardless of the weather than in the fact that it makes it possible to apply that moisture just when and just where it is needed. For instance, on some cloudless day the strawberry patch looks thirsty and cries for water through the unmistakable language of its leaves. In the Atlantic States it probably would not rain that day, such is the perversity of nature, but if it did it would rain alike on the just and unjust—on the strawberries, which would be benefited by it, and on the sugar-beets, which crave only the uninterrupted sunshine that they may pack their tiny cells with saccharine matter. In the arid region there is practically no rain during the growing season. Thus the scientific farmer sends the water from his canal through the little furrows which divide the lines of strawberry plants, but permits the water to go singing past his field of beets.

—*Smythe*

II

TRANSFORMING THE DESERT[1]

Our Growth by Internal Development

One of the most far-reaching home-making efforts of our history was little thought of in 1899. By 1905 it was in full swing. Within that short space of six years interest in it multiplied a thousand fold. Our greatest national conquests are not external, but those of our natural resources. A prime essential to national greatness is internal development. Had this been practised by China in the same proportion as in the United States, we, with all our advancement, would by comparison be a pygmy nation. Industrial preeminence was first achieved in New England, one of our most unfavorable sections; but the mastery of conditions so stubborn prepared our countrymen for larger conquests westward, where our first

---

[1] Our indebtedness to Smythe, *The Conquest of Arid America*, and to other sources is at times so indirect that this general acknowledgment will in most cases cover all later references, except where quotations are made. The citation of magazines, under REFERENCES FOR FURTHER STUDY, at the close of chapters may also largely answer the double purpose of reference and giving of credit.

national lessons were learned and the kind of tasks found which developed the learners for what followed. These were not accidental; God was in them all.

Expansion Through Regular Agriculture

By ordinary agricultural methods thirty-two states were added to the original thirteen. Our national population was increased fourteen fold and our cities came to rival the world's greatest urban centers. According to the census of 1900, we had nearly ten and a half millions of people engaged in agriculture, with a total approaching five and three quarters millions of separate farms. During the ten years ending with 1900, we added in farms an extent nearly equal to that of France and Germany.

Interrelation of Factors

Our civilization rests upon agriculture. It is the basis of manufactures. Agriculture and manufactures are interdependent. Railroads depend on both. Any considerable enlargement of our agricultural area touches most vitally our national life and acts directly upon all our interests. It quickens equally the pulse of Church life and missionary endeavor.

Irrigation

Broad Bearings of Irrigation

Irrigation is not a local affair. Every acre of land, in any part of the United States, re-

UNITED STATES
(PHYSICAL)

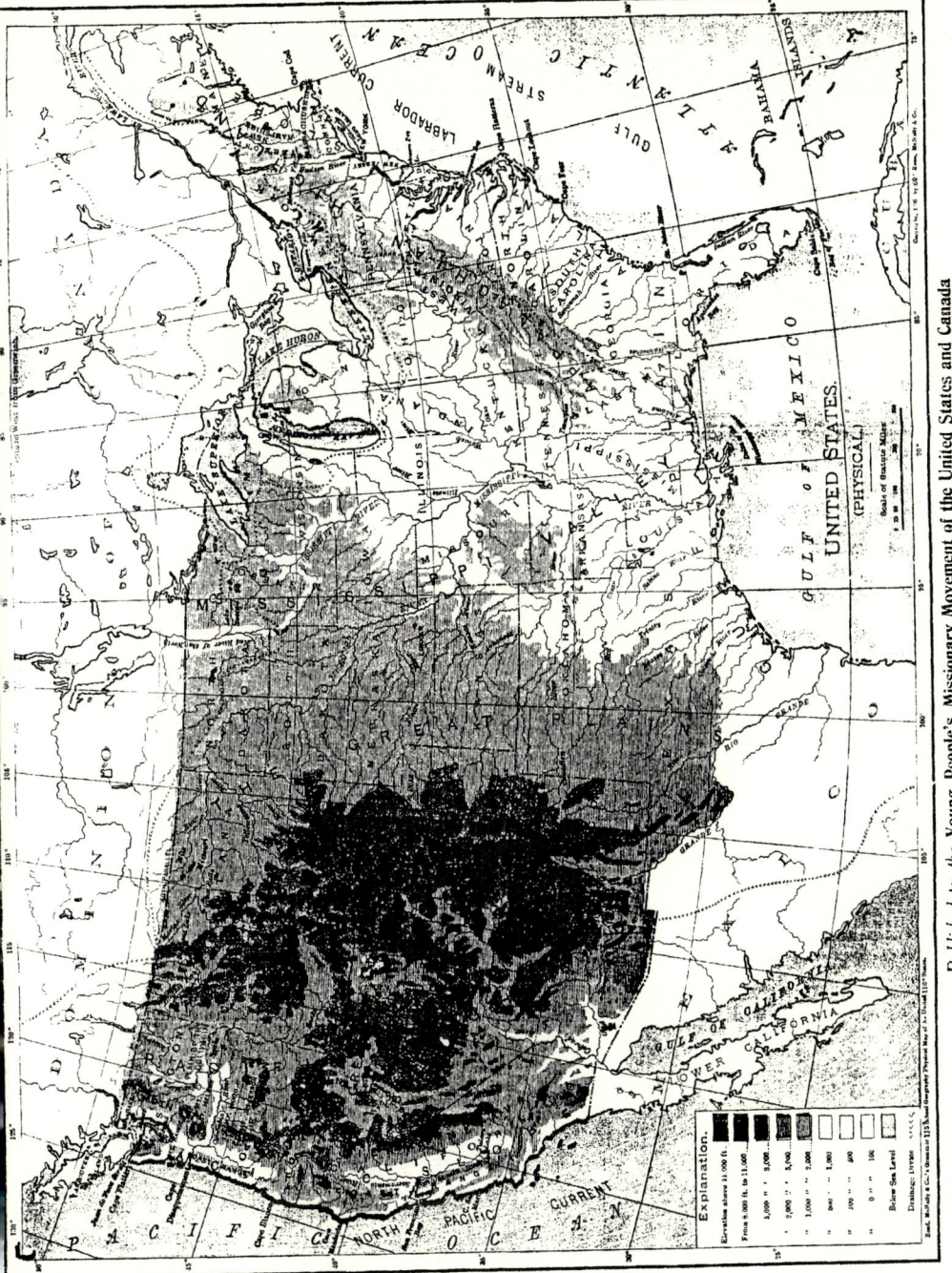

Published by the Young People's Missionary Movement of the United States and Canada

claimed and made productive sooner or later touches all industries and every moral issue East or West.

East of the 97th degree of west longitude lies one half the territory of the United States, where live nine tenths of our people. The one half west of the 97th degree is the better of the two and capable of maintaining a population much greater than the present total of the whole country. **Two Sections Contrasted**

The dominant motive for western emigration is home making. This gives stability to each advance, for the home is perennial. This westward migration paused not until it crossed the 97th degree. It there met aridity. With grim determination the settlers faced an enigma, a climate then inscrutable. They faltered and retreated. And now we learn that aridity is a blessing. It was the alphabet of ancient prosperity. Beyond the 97th meridian live not very many more people than in the single state of New York. We rub our eyes with a new awakening, and to-morrow, more even than to-day, great tides of homesteaders will be pressing, with unquestioning confidence, across this once inhospitable frontier. **New Phase of Aridity**

Our Western Table-land

A relief map of the United States is a revelation. A glance shows why the West, our frontier, so differs from the East. At the 97th degree, which is not far from the western boundary line of Minnesota, the country begins gradually to rise, until when it reaches about the 103d meridian it looks, from there on to the Pacific, like a jumbled mass of mountains and valleys. The whole with its varying altitudes is a high table-land. This accounts for a climate of such marked contrast to that of the East. In some places its farms and cities stand fully a mile above sea-level.

Mountain Ranges and Desert Section

Midway and diagonally across this western frontier extend the Rocky Mountains. Inland from the Pacific coast are the Cascade and Sierra ranges. These last are of such height as to intercept the clouds moving eastward and rob them of their moisture. Thus on the east side of these mountains we have skies almost cloudless, an atmosphere clear and bracing, and a consequent dryness which has produced a desert landscape mostly uninhabited.

How Can We Tame This Desert?

The taming of this desert has presented obstacles so new to us that until within the last few years the nation has not, in any large way, set itself to their removal. We have been forced to this, because the public lands open to settlers are mostly exhausted; that is, lands where homes may be made under normal conditions.

Previous Abundance of Land with Rainfall

Heretofore our domain has furnished acres in abundance where rainfall is assured. It was necessary only that a citizen of the United States "file his claim" for one hundred and sixty acres of land, live on the same for a comparatively brief period, make certain inexpensive improvements, and the land was his. This has been an outlet to congested populations and a foundation of our national wealth. About one third of the land of the United States, however, has not passed into private ownership, but of that one third not more than five acres in a hundred can be tilled without irrigation. Millions of acres await settlement in a country largely rainless.

Aridity and Its Advantage

In eastern portions of the United States we have a rainfall of fifty or more inches per annum. This is also true of the extreme Northwest. In parts of these humid sections the difficulty of disposing of surplus water about equals irrigation problems on the western plains. Any portion of the country where the rainfall is less than twenty inches per annum is termed arid. There are portions of the United States where the amount is not half that. Aridity has been spoken of as the great resource of the West. This seems contradictory, but we are reminded that from choice great civilizations of the past were in arid regions. In the Bible water is spoken of as in an irrigated country. The Book opens and closes with a river. Christ presents himself as the water of life.

An Inexhaustibly Fertile Soil

In our arid West the one element which gives value is water. A peculiarity of an arid region is its soil. It is seemingly barren, yet an analysis of the soil of our western deserts shows a marvelous natural richness. The application of water works wonderful transformations. Products in quality and quantity are amazing. The soil in these dry climates has never been impoverished. Its valuable mineral constituents have not been dissolved and washed out by rains. These elements of fertility under irrigation accumulate rather than lessen.

Intensive Farming

The Nile valley is cited as an example of enrichment caused for ages by the overflowing of the Nile River. These benefits are ascribed to a sediment left on the land. This deposit,

RAISING GRAPES IN THE SALT RIVER
VALLEY, NEAR MESA, ARIZONA

DATE TREE IN SALT RIVER VALLEY
NEAR MESA, ARIZONA

Transforming the Desert

however, is so slight as to make it certain that the soil does not draw its productiveness from that source. It is inherent in aridity. Thus the land of arid regions, when once brought under irrigation, possesses possibilities easily in excess of acres in humid regions. This admits of intensive farming. Bright sunshine is a constant asset. The farmer does not wait for the rain any more than he waits to plow. He plants without interruption from inclement weather, and then scientifically applies moisture according to the various needs of his growing crops. It is estimated that with this culture one to two acres per person will render a comfortable livelihood. In other words, five to forty acres will better care for an average family than four to five times that amount in parts of the country where agriculture depends on rainfall.

As one passes southward he finds that in a single season irrigation produces a series of crops. The soil is not exhausted and is not fertilized. A Series of Crops

Features of the Problem

This whole dry table-land is in extent from north to south about equal to the distance from Extent of Table-land

Montreal to Mobile, and from east to west it would reach from Boston to Omaha, yet, as we have before noted, it has no navigable river, save for short distances, other than the Missouri.

Transient Streams and Canyon Formation

Lack of forests fails to restrain what rainfall there is. It comes rushing down seamed declivities, and fills dry beds of streams which for a brief time become swollen torrents tearing out great quantities of earth and rock. This results in canyon formations, the most marvelous of which is the Grand Canyon of the Colorado. The Colorado River, a creature of such fitful conditions, presents in itself a study and history most unique. It is said to be the most observed river in the world.

Some Results of Private Enterprise

These streams and rivers, in various parts of the western table-land, by private enterprise have been diverted into irrigation ditches until millions of acres have been reclaimed. In the Southwest these ditches have followed the models furnished by a prehistoric race, traces of whose irrigation schemes, agricultural prosperity, and marvelous cities are the wonder of the world. Possibilities of this kind of irrigation, however, have largely been exhausted. Corporations have inaugurated ambitious undertakings, but these, in a number of cases, have proved unprofitable to the investors, as the land cannot well bear the expense of a water system above the actual cost of construction.

One great work yet remained, the control of rivers and streams at their sources, by creating immense storage dams, from which water, taken in flood tide, when needed later, might gradually replenish the channels of irrigation.

Control of Streams at Their Sources

Governmental Action Necessary

The cost of such stupendous engineering feats is beyond private capital. Hence, the government has undertaken this work. At present, in different parts of the West, north and south, it has so far completed eleven great plants as to furnish water for five hundred thousand acres of land. It has under way and in contemplation a number of other schemes which will add an acreage several times as large as that already reclaimed. There is not water sufficient to reclaim anything like all the land of the arid West, but possibilities in that direction are estimated as high as one hundred million acres. This means ideal homes for from fifteen to twenty millions of people.

Limits of the System

Provision for Irrigation Fund

Our national Congress in 1902 enacted one of the most statesmanlike provisions ever framed for the creation of millions of homes.[1] It set apart the proceeds from the sale of public lands in the various states to the credit of each. This is the basis of an irrigation fund which has reached a total of more than forty-one millions of dollars. The cost of surveying and constructing a great irrigation scheme in any given state is charged against the amount to its credit. The cost is spread equally over the acreage reclaimed and is paid by the settlers in ten equal instalments without interest. The money is a revolving fund used again and again to extend irrigation. At the end of the ten years the land, with the inherent water rights, belongs to the homesteader who meanwhile enjoys the proceeds of his farm. He must, however, actually live upon the land and cultivate it. He can own in most cases not more than from forty to eighty acres. This prevents speculation and insures the aim of the government—the establishment of homes. Whoever lives upon one of these allotments of land is as sure of a comfortable livelihood as he is of running water. The mountains feed

[1] See Appendix E.

these sources of supply and make the streams perennial.

Another recent remarkable discovery is that, underlying great stretches of our western country where water from streams is not available, are vast underground lakes. These have made possible thousands of artesian wells, some of which flow with sufficient volume to irrigate one hundred and sixty acres each. *Underground Lakes and Artesian Wells*

Water in connection with irrigation plants may have other uses than application to the soil. Flowing through sluiceways or pipes it may have so great a fall that when striking a water-wheel it is converted into tremendous power which in turn may be utilized in pumping the waters of the same dam to lands on higher levels. Again this power makes possible factories and various manufactories. It is converted into electricity, in which form it is transferred to distant points for light and power. Sometimes it has occurred that in the construction of a great irrigation dam in the desert the activities of the builders have continued night and day, the works being brilliantly lighted during the night with electricity born of the wilderness waters. *Water-power Results*

Purposeful Young Manhood

Praise for the Engineers

Most people have little conception of the heroism, self-sacrifice, and persistency displayed by the young men of this country in their astonishing feats of engineering in connection with building western irrigation plants. They have been obliged to survey and build government roads where it was impossible for a human being to get a foothold. They have been suspended by ropes over yawning chasms into which they were let down and whose shadowy depths they have explored, where later, blasting from solid cliffs, they have built leagues of government road over whose edge a stone may be dropped a sheer fall of a thousand feet.

Conquering All Obstacles

An engineer with his assistants was running a surveyor's line when he encountered a towering rock cliff which caused him to suspend operations with the remark, "I must stop and think." It was seemingly to think squarely against the impossible, as there was no apparent way around or over the mountain of rock. When he learned that this unconquered obstacle would cause a loop of fifteen added miles to the road he decided to go straight on and the road was built.[1] Where a mountain is in the road of the contemplated flow of a stream, the mountain is tunneled for miles. In short, nothing seems insurmountable to this generation of Uncle Sam's young men.

This is a life-chapter that the young people of this country should know more about. These scores and hundreds of trained young men, who have fought their way to the front, with many more who are their helpers, are in scores of isolated places in the United States, heroes in a great cause which they enthusiastically serve. They contribute trained efforts and lives to one of the greatest missionary movements ever launched on the American continent, which is the reclaiming of the desert and peopling it with millions in comfortable homes, surrounded by manifold opportunities and uplifting influences. These multitudes, save for this ministry, might otherwise never rise above the dreary horizon of grinding subsistence. *A Striking Life-chapter*

Irrigation dams are built in various forms, conforming to the topography and needs of localities. The task may be to close the narrow mouth of a rocky canyon by building a dam higher than the Flatiron building in New *Irrigation Dams and New Waterways*

---
[1] Blanchard, *National Geographic Magazine*, April, 1908.

York City, or on lower levels to construct barriers of great length, thereby producing the largest artificial lakes known in the world. These new waterways are, to some extent, navigable.

Creation of Towns and Missionary Opportunity

The towns which spring up in these hitherto uninhabited regions are substantial and prosperous. Their sudden appearance and rapid development are marvelous. While the dam is building, houses are erected on nearly every allotment, still a barren waste. A chief officer of the reclamation service tells how, about three or four years ago, he slept at night on a sagebrush desert thirty miles from a human habitation. An assistant sketched for him on the lone sands a plan of a town which, in that inhospitable solitude, seemed a satire, yet, it was not so long afterward that this official, in visiting that locality, found a town of hundreds of inhabitants with a bank and other structures in keeping with a growing community. Where, on his previous visit, his camp had been, now stood the school building of the town. This is not mushroom growth. It is based on irrigated farm lands, than which there is no source of livelihood more sure and substantial. What missionary opportunities in our country are thus being opened up! What communities will now be needing both church and pastor! These people must be helped. They invest all in getting started. Not the least of the ministries which will make these new neighborhoods beautiful and fruitful in spiritual and temporal things may be the daily lives of our young people, who there will find it possible to transplant into their new homes the high ideals and purposes which were born in other surroundings.

An Ideal Social Order

The social order resulting from government irrigation is to have its influence on American life. It creates a democratic and coöperative condition of living as opposed to the individualistic. One, in a country of abundant rainfall, living on a vast estate, can foster the individualistic spirit and exist, but in a community of small holdings, entirely dependent upon a single irrigation plant, into which is merged the collective material prosperity of the whole community, the individualistic spirit succumbs to the coöperative and the democratic. This is the fairest flower that springs from irrigated soil.

Social Type

Sparse Population a Drawback

In a humid region one may secure a farm covering thousands of acres. This he may devote to various forms of agriculture; or in a semiarid country miles of territory may come under the ownership of a single man and may be devoted to wheat raising or grazing; this, however, means a population so sparse that whole counties are left comparatively uninhabited. Progress, social development, and the betterment of the many are foreign to such conditions.

Contrast Under Irrigation

The government irrigation scheme reverses all this. It places limitations upon the amount of land held by the individual. The limitations of nature are yet more imperative, as a small farm under irrigation means prosperity, a large one calamity. The allotments of land are of such few acres—in many cases but forty, twenty, or ten—that the face of the country is transformed from a desert waste or a solitary cattle-range into a landscape thickly dotted with homes. The tendency is to group the dwellings, to connect them with modern appliances of water system, telephone, free mail delivery, and other conveniences; in short, to make them the acme of ideal residence towns for the people. These delectable conditions are

BUILDING HOMES IN ANTICIPATION OF THE OPENING OF GOVERNMENT WORKS
ARIZONA

HOME NEAR PHOENIX, ARIZONA, SHOWING WHAT IRRIGATION WILL DO FOR THE DESERT

Transforming the Desert

further enhanced when a series of such communities are connected by an electrical railway system. The social and Christian meaning of all this needs little enlargement.

One person living in the midst of six hundred and forty acres or of four thousand acres, or nobody living in vast desert stretches, means a correspondingly slight obligation on the part of the Church; but when the six hundred and forty acres or the four thousand acres have a home on every forty, twenty, or ten acre division, and when the wilderness comes to support a teeming population, then the Church faces a virgin field where social, industrial, educational, and, most of all, spiritual realities await its guiding hand. These communities offer unique opportunities. Take for example Riverside, California, one of the earlier communities born of irrigation. One is struck by the large number of homes admirably situated and attractive in appearance. He may be suprised to learn that these are the dwellings of people who, were they living in other places, might be less desirably situated. This is because the few acres belonging to each family afford an income secure and unfailing. They are not subject to uncertain fluctuations

Desirable Home Conditions

that might attend them under other conditions. This means homes with all that word implies. A commonwealth is neither less nor more than the homes of its people.

Highest Average, East and West

It may be suggestive to remark that Rhode Island, our most thickly settled state, is able to support something more than five hundred people per square mile, while in the irrigated district of California to which reference has been made we have more than twice that number for each square mile.

Religious Aspect

Fascinating Field for the Church

When we consider the various sections of the arid West which are now, because of irrigation, undergoing rapid transformation, and where in the next few years will spring up hundreds of new towns and thickly settled neighborhoods, our pulse beats quicker with the thrill of what awaits a Church which to-day enters the gateway of a field so fascinating.

Potential Promoters of the Kingdom

These many coming centers of pulsating life and possible spiritual power will, if properly cared for in their inception, be among our most fruitful sources both of money and personal investment for the foreign field. They may yet furnish for the kingdom abundant means, intelligence, and spiritual life for the world's greatest need.

Forests

Another feature of the West illustrates how all nature, when properly interpreted and operated for the highest good of man, is coördinate with God's kingdom in the earth. Streams and rivers cannot be conserved for irrigation if sufficient forest lands are not preserved. The springs gushing out in these shaded recesses disappear when exposed to searching sunlight. The rainfall, plentiful in the mountains, likewise the melting masses of snow, are held back by fallen forest leaves and masses of undergrowth and the accumulated mold of centuries. The streams which rise there emerge upon the plains with a steady, continuous flow. However, when the mountains have been denuded of forest covering, the waters sweep down their unobstructed sides. Streams become raging rivers. Rivers in a night rise to a flood, and the beneficent moisture which might have been evenly distributed for many days, precipitates a calamity. It washes off great stretches of fertile soil and covers productive acres with deposits of barren rock and gravel. The waters are as swift in

Function of Forests

subsiding as in coming. Ruin is in their wake and the agriculturist is left without resources for future crops.

Destruction of Forests Unnecessary

The slaughter of our forests has been wanton.[1] At the present rate, within from thirty to fifty years, our most valuable timber supply will be exhausted. This, from the commercial standpoint, cannot be supplied by South America and other countries, as they do not possess a marketable substitute for our most useful woods. These forests were designed by the Creator as an inheritance for many generations. No mere land title confers upon any one a divine right ruthlessly to destroy the sources of subsistence and comfort for the many. Forests properly managed will produce an adequate supply of timber practically undiminished.

Among the Essentials of Life

Our forests may be classed with soil, water, and bread, as indispensable to life. Older countries where forests have been destroyed are in part a desolation. In other words, we can have little running water, productive soil, or bread without the forests.

Forests at Head Waters

One hundred and sixty-five millions of acres of forest and adjacent woodlands, out of the

---

[1] Hough, *Everybody's Magazine*, May, 1908.

total public reserve, have been set apart by the government for the public good. Special attention is given to the enlargement of wood areas from which spring the head waters of streams of the arid West.

At the head of the forestry department is a remarkable man.[1] He, with an army of enthusiastic helpers, among them many of our young men, is guarding, replenishing, and creating our forest reserve. Thus it comes about that the government forest reserve and the government irrigation scheme are inseparable, and that the silent trees on the distant mountainsides, where the sound of the human voice is seldom heard, are linked in a gracious conspiracy with the streams that play about their roots to create and maintain on the distant sun-parched plains a fulfilment of the purpose of their Creator. "The wilderness and the dry land shall be glad; and the desert shall rejoice, and blossom as the rose."

Efforts to Maintain Our Forest Reserves

Governmental Attitude

The aim of the government is not rapidly to dispose of our public lands, but to utilize them

Far-reaching Plans

---

[1] Barnes, "Gifford Pinchot, Forester." *McClure's Magazine.* July, 1908.

in such a manner as may best tend to the creation of homes for the greatest number of people. Hence, these far-reaching and extensive plans inaugurated in very recent years.

President Roosevelt's Interest

The early training of President Roosevelt on a western ranch gave him practical experience and quick understanding in these important matters. He says, "The forest and water problems are, perhaps, the most vital internal questions of the United States." This whole subject, in the government reports and other literature springing from it, is among the fascinating reading of the day.

Irrigation and Adjacent Pasture-lands

Irrigation is having an important influence upon great stretches of adjacent lands the topography of which prevents the application of water. This land is covered with a scanty vegetation peculiar to the arid country. It offers fairly good subsistence to cattle.

Breaking up of Great Cattle-ranges

But the government now forbids the fencing in of the public domain; thus the cattle cannot legally be confined on public lands. The cattle owners are responsible for damages to others, consequently the great ranges are being broken up.

Cattle Industry Passing Into Many Hands

The number of cattle supplied to the markets does not, however, decrease. The farmers on the arable lands, by arrangement with the government, secure the right to turn their cattle upon adjoining public lands. This fosters the making of homes, and the farmer from his irrigated acres, or as a result of dry farming, produces forage sufficient to furnish his cattle a substitute for wide grazing. Thus the cattle industry, more and more, passes into the hands of many rather than the few, and intensive and dry farming come to have an influence on the whole West much more extensive than the mere acres under cultivation.

Dry Farming

Dry farming is producing marked changes in the West. This, in any large way, has not been understood and practised, until in the last few years. Where conditions permit, it now has been taken into all the western states and territories. The method is adapted to a region where rainfall is deficient and water for irrigation is not available. <small>A New Method</small>

The method is to begin as early as possible in the spring by plowing. The soil is then rolled and harrowed. No crop should be planted the first season. After every important rain the ground is harrowed with the <small>Process for the First Season</small>

twofold purpose of keeping a soil mulch on the surface and killing out weeds. This soil mulch prevents moisture escaping from below and it keeps the soil open to receive the rains instead of permitting them to run off as on a hard surface.

Steps Till Crop is Secured

Early in the fall the ground is plowed again; then packed, harrowed, and seeded to winter wheat. In the spring these wheat-fields are rolled and harrowed several times until the wheat is so high that it practically shades the ground. As soon as the grain is harvested the soil is disked,[1] creating again a mulch which prevents rapid evaporation from the surface which has been shaded during several weeks of hot weather. The second spring this field is double-disked as early as possible, plowed, harrowed, packed, and a variety of crops is planted. During growth the harrow is used freely. By this method fair returns are secured from lands heretofore considered comparatively worthless.[2]

Increasing Rains in the Semiarid Belt

Extending down through North and South Dakota, Kansas, Nebraska, Oklahoma, and

---

[1] Treated with a farm implement made up of revolving disks.

[2] See Deming, *Independent*, April 18, 1907.

Texas, to the Gulf, is a belt two hundred or more miles wide termed semiarid. In this area, especially in the northern part, many new settlers experienced in the early nineties a few years of most distressing drought and famine. Those who were not able to retreat eastward and those who were courageous enough to stay, endured hardships the like of which are seldom experienced in this country on so large a scale over a region so extensive. Numbers had pushed beyond the semiarid belt into that which is termed arid. This whole frontier was reckoned as beyond the limit where man could subsist by agriculture without irrigation. The hardy pioneers, however, who endured these unfavorable conditions for a very few years were at last encouraged by increasing rains, and until the present, no period or single year has at all resembled the earlier years and hardships mentioned.

The system of dry farming is practised to a large extent. Homesteaders in greater numbers than ever are settling up the once abandoned claims or pushing westward into regions hitherto unoccupied, making homes there and witnessing the growth of inviting new settlements.

Homesteaders Entering the Dry Farming Region

Call to the Churches

Fields for Home Mission Effort

Taken as a whole, the great arid West and its past development as a field for the Church is a sufficient pledge of its future as a Christian domain. Irrigation changes western lands into gardens, and orchards wave where sagebrush flourished. Whole populations are deposited over wide stretches of territory and the insistent call is for scores of our brightest young people to enter thousands of fast ripening harvest-fields.

Starting with the People

A pastor under date of 1908 tells how he started work on the Minidoka government irrigation project. "You ask for something about Idaho, and how I came to be there? Well, once upon a time, in 1906, my wife and I were spending our August vacation at Gato, where the Colorado Assembly is held. In the shade of the old pine tree the 'evangelist' told us of ———, Idaho, a town just started, and a new church of forty members. The pioneer blood in our veins gave a start, and, although we had 'glittering prospects,' six months later found us on a sagebrush claim, in the midst of the great Minidoka government irrigation project of one hundred and sixty thousand acres. Our mansion, like most of our neighbors, is a board shack lined with building-paper. The twenty-two hundred dollar church built by those forty members was the largest and practically the first permanent building on the whole project. But my, how poor every one of us was! Right away I was doing carpenter work, with a gang of men, for the government, while preaching on Sundays. It was camping out and vacation all the time.

"Our first year is just completed and the forty have grown to sixty-five. During the year we raised about thirteen hundred dollars, one hundred and twenty-five of which was for missions. I challenge any other church in the brotherhood, worth financially four times as much per member, to show as much work done in the year 1907, financially and otherwise, considering the size of the membership as the ———— church.

Record of a Year

"I admit that the vacation phase of the situation has worn off. The sacrificing reaches almost to the quick sometimes. So far the Board has only been able to help by giving us a meeting with the state evangelist. Without more help we thought we should have to go, but we are still here, and still hoping for help.

Keen Self-sacrifice

And how can we leave? It's true we think of larger things sometimes. But where is a larger need or as large-hearted a people as here?

Workings of the Irrigation System

"This great tract of rich fruit and grain land is divided into forty and eighty acre claims. It is already much more thickly settled than farming communities in Iowa or Nebraska. Its settlers are young people from the Middle West, the most enlightened class I have ever seen in any community. Uncle Sam has built a perfect irrigation system, allowing the people ten years in which to pay for it. Land in these parts on projects two years older than this one is actually selling for from sixty to three hundred dollars per acre. There are four other tracts similar to this one in southeastern Idaho now under construction, a vast empire containing some of the richest soil in the country.

Plea for Prompt Action

"Our Secretary simply does not dare organize new churches, for he cannot promise financial aid from the board to help support the minister. I plead with our people, who are no less able and no less generous-hearted than others, that *now* is the time to come to the rescue of our work in this great country, born full-grown."

Transforming the Desert

Such types of people will not yield to the ministrations of poorly equipped, ordinary agencies. The prairie schooner and the prairie schooner method are both belated. New frontier cities throbbing with life so tense and abundant will harken to no hesitating prophet, and will be transformed to the city of God by no half-way measures. In no age of our American history has there sounded a clearer call, one freighted with larger issues, than that now summoning the choicest young people of the Church to give themselves to our unfolding frontier.

Imperial Call of the Unfolding Frontier

QUESTIONS FOR CHAPTER II

AIM: TO SHOW HOW NEW METHODS IN AGRICULTURE HAVE INCREASED THE CALL FOR MISSION WORK ON THE FRONTIER

1.* Name the commercial enterprises that are dependent upon agriculture.
2.* Could America be a world power without great agricultural resources? Give reasons.
3. Tell just how you are dependent upon agriculture daily.
4. Why do more people in agricultural districts own their homes than in cities?
5.* Do you believe that rural life encourages home-making more than urban life? Give reasons.
6. Where are you apt to find the more democratic spirit, in the country or in the city? Give reasons.

7. In proportion to numbers where will you find superior moral conditions, in the city or country?
8. Name several methods by which the water is controlled and directed in irrigation systems.
9. Describe the method of irrigating a small farm.
10. What sections of the world have in the past employed irrigation? Name some foreign countries that are now developing irrigation systems.
11.* Would you prefer to own and work a farm that is irrigated or one dependent on rainfall? Give reasons.
12. What benefits accrue to the soil from irrigation?
13. Why is it possible to support a larger agricultural population in an irrigated section than in a section which depends upon rainfall?
14.* Would you prefer to engage in general mercantile business in an irrigated section or in a section dependent upon rainfall? Why?
15. Do you believe that our government should continue to assist in extending irrigation? Why?
16. What commercial evils does the Irrigation Fund prevent?
17.* Name some of the benefits that result to land from forests.
18. Why do you believe that the government should protect our forests?
19. Name some country that has made rapid progress in forestry.
20. Describe clearly the method of dry farming.

21. Do you believe that this method of agriculture will ever be equal in productiveness to irrigation? Give reasons.
22.* Name some difficulties in the establishment of churches among cattle-ranges.
23. What classes of men usually follow the vocation of cowboys?
24. Why is it easier to establish a church in an irrigated section?
25. What class of people usually inhabit these new agricultural sections?
26. Name some social ideals that are a result of irrigated communities.
27. Do you believe that a larger force of home missionaries is now needed under these rapidly changing conditions on the frontier?
28. Has your home missionary society been able to increase its budget in proportion to the increased opportunities on the frontier? Why not?
29. What can you do to increase gifts to work on the frontier?

REFERENCES FOR FURTHER STUDY
CHAPTER II[1]

I. *Irrigation.*[2]

Anderson: "Irrigation in Southwestern United States and Mexico." Out West, August, '06.

---

[1] For additional reference, see Bibliography, pages 265-279 of this book. The current magazies should also be consulted for more recent articles on these subjects.

[2] Send to Government Reclamation Service, Washington, D. C., tor literature on Irrigation.

Beacom: "Irrigation in the United States; Its Geographical and Economical Results." Geographical Journal, April, '07.

Cope: "Making Gardens Out of Lava-dust." World To-day, June, '06.

Deming: "Irrigation in Wyoming." Independent, May 9, '07.

Page: "The Rediscovery of Our Greatest Wealth." World's Work, May, '08.

Smythe: The Conquest of Arid America, Part I, Chapter IV; Part II, Chapters III, IV.

Taylor: "Agriculture by Irrigation; Economic Problems in Irrigation." Journal of Political Economy, April, '07.

II. *Dry Farming.*

Cowan: "Dry Farming the Hope of the West." Century, July, '06.

Deming: "Dry Farming; What It Is." Independent, April 18, '07.

Donahue: "Farming Without Water." World Today, August, '06.

Quick: "Farming Without Water." World's Work, August, '06.

III. *Forestry.*

Blackwelder: "A Country that has Used up Its Trees." Outlook, March, '06.

Fernow: "Saving the Waste of Forests." Country Life in America, August, '07.

Geiser: "Results of Forestry in Germany." World's Work, March, '07.

Roosevelt: "Forest and Reclamation Service of the United States." National Geographic Magazine, November, '06.

Sterling: "Reforestation in Southern California." Out West, July, '07.

Will: "Forestry; Planting Trees for Profit." World's Work, November, '07.

THE GIANT NORTHWEST

Mr. James J. Hill has said of his controlling ambition:

"I have been charged with everything, from being an 'Oriental dreamer' to a crank, but I am ready at all times to plead guilty to any intelligent effort within my power that will result in getting new markets for what we produce in the northwestern country."

He has made his dreams come true. Seattle was a straggling seaside town when he put his railroad into it. Since that time the Puget Sound ports have become mighty rivals of San Francisco for ocean traffic, and the older city at the Golden Gate has seen them increase their tonnage by leaps and bounds, and at her expense.

—Paine

The whole country traversed through the northern tier of territories, from Eastern Dakota to Washington, is a habitable region. For the entire distance every square mile of the country is valuable either for farming, stock-raising, or timber-cutting. There is absolutely no waste land between the well-settled region of Dakota and the new wheat region of Washington. Even on the tops of the Rocky Mountains there is good pasturage; and the vast timber belt enveloping Clark's Fork and Lake Pend d'Oreille, and the ranges of the Cabinet and Cœur d'Alene Mountains, is more valuable than an equal extent of arable land.

—Smalley

III

THE GIANT NORTHWEST[1]

Either North or South Dakota is as large as New England. Montana, the third largest state in the Union, nearly equals in size Japan, or England, Ireland, Scotland, and Wales, with twenty-five thousand square miles to spare, or it nearly equals New England, New York, and Pennsylvania. An express train crossing it from east to west needs more than the daylight hours. Washington dwarfs some eastern states but Oregon is about equal to Washington and Maine. Idaho would reach from Toronto to Raleigh, North Carolina. New England and the middle states would need duplicating several times to cover these northwest states as a whole.

Comparisons of Extent

The Northwest Is a Giant in Possibilities

We have defined the western frontier to be

Steps of Approach

---

[1] Under this title we group the states of North and South Dakota, Montana, Idaho, Washington, and Oregon. Wyoming is also geographically related, but because of its physical features it falls more naturally into the next chapter.

considered by us as the territory west of the 97th meridian. We noted that for the most part it is an arid plateau with physical features and climate in sharp contrast to the country eastward. We have pointed out how Providence has placed us geographically in the zone of world power, how the early explorers found waterways convenient for westward exploration, and how the first Pacific coast American civilization was planted by missionaries in the Puget Sound region of the Northwest. We have followed the hardy frontiersmen in their western progress, and now let us learn something of the meaning of all this.

Puget Sound and Its Connections Puget Sound is the only harbor north of the Golden Gate equal to a world commerce. It is one of the most marvelous inland waterways on the continent, with its 1,600 miles of coastline, it opens into the sea with a passage so wide and deep that any vessel afloat in any weather may pass freely in and out. Its waters, up to the very shores, are mostly of such depth that ships may anchor under the shade of trees. A steamer leaving it for China would reach port two days sooner than from San Francisco because of the shorter curvature of the earth. It is near the Columbia River pass, the only open-

SECOND AVENUE AND CHERRY STREET, SEATTLE, WASHINGTON

ing cutting the Coast Range nearly to sea level. This corresponds to the gateway to the Atlantic seaboard through the Appalachian Range, formed by the Mohawk and Hudson Rivers.

As a seaport for Oriental trade, in addition to the shorter ocean voyage, Puget Sound is five hundred miles nearer Chicago by rail than is San Francisco. On freight shipped from Chicago it has then an advantage over San Francisco harbor equal to about the distance from Buffalo to Chicago plus the ascent of Pike's Peak; for all the overland freight to San Francisco must be lifted up and let down again ten thousand feet in crossing the Coast Range, while at Puget Sound it crosses at about sea-level.[1]

On the Favored Route Orientward

Trade, like water, takes the channel of least resistance. Thus Puget Sound is destined as our gateway to the Orient. In time it may be cheaper for San Francisco to receive and send her eastern freight by the way of the Northwest as the intervening mountains of the present railways eastward are too great to be tunneled. Portland harbor is nearer the Columbia River pass eastward than is Puget Sound, but

Our Gateway to the Far East

---

[1] See Thomas, "Our Own Northwest." *Success Magazine*, October and November, 1907.

the bar at the mouth of the Columbia is a menace to the largest ocean liners, and in storm there is no protection for vessels waiting to enter. The two hundred mile stretch from Portland to Puget Sound is almost a floor level. A ship-canal from Portland to Puget Sound is more than possible. Cities on and contiguous to this harbor promise to be among the greatest in the world.

The Northwest Is a Giant in Natural Resources

Resources Contiguous to This Center

Clustering about Puget Sound are many natural sources of supply for the Orient. The most extensive forests on earth center there. One lumber firm in a single shipment sent out twenty steamers with cargoes of lumber ranging from three and a quarter millions to about four millions of feet each. Puget Sound touches one of the most productive agricultural regions in the world. The fruits grown there in quality and quantity are unexcelled. Steamer fuel is found in coal deposits near the harbor.

Diversified Products

The Columbia gateway eastward opens into a depression termed "The Inland Empire"—the Spokane country. It covers most of eastern Washington and a part of northern Oregon. You can drop New England here with room to spare. It is a grain and fruit producing country. It pours out millions upon millions of bushels of wheat for the Orient. Idaho is tributary to the Puget Sound port with its mines, lumber, and agriculture. Montana is changing from cattle ranges to farms. The last open range is in the northeastern part of the state, but in five years it will be no more. Montana is becoming an agricultural state. Its famous Gallatin Valley produces a quality of grain sought by makers of cereal foods. Billings probably ships more wool than any other inland point in the world. Its million dollar sugar-beet factory is the largest in the United States. Montana now raises as much corn per acre as Iowa. The western parts of North and South Dakota have become veritable bread-baskets of the earth.

The Northwest Is a Giant in Achievement

In every state of the Northwest, in addition to private enterprises, the government has constructed or has under way irrigation plants that reclaim hundreds of thousands of acres. This means intensive farming. Ten acres of irrigated orchard in some sections is worth six hundred and forty acres of ordinary grain land.

Development in Intensive and Dry Farming

This insures for all time vast shipments to Asia by Puget Sound. Dry farming is reclaiming millions of acres and still further swelling the tide of breadstuffs to the Far East.

Seed Selection and Viviculture

Seed selection and viviculture are also working wonders. The agricultural college is a world asset. A professor in Iowa evolved seed that increased the corn crop of his state ten bushels to the acre. In a North Dakota College is a German professor, still in his early forties, an immigrant, who ranks next to Burbank in contributions to the vegetable kingdom.

Fruit Acquisitions

The Russian winters of the Northwest, east of the Rockies, are invigorating to man, but death to small fruits and orchards. This professor brooded over the numberless northwestern homes lacking in fruit comforts. He patiently applied himself, and now luscious strawberries, raspberries, and cherries grow there, which without protection do not kill out at forty degrees below zero.

Acclimated Alfalfa

He is at work on other fruits, including apples. A hardy decorative foliage-bush is now produced and roses are on the way. His three journeys to Asia, in tracing alfalfa northward, are among the heroic feats of history. He said in a college chapel service he thought that he was doing the Lord's work. One can hardly compute what an acclimated alfalfa may mean to the Northwest.

Already its corn has been made to germinate at lower and lower temperatures until its season for ripening has been lengthened two weeks. Not only does Asia promise to enrich the Northwest with alfalfa, but she has already furnished it with her durum and macaroni wheat, adapted to dry uplands, and where sown it has thereby increased the yield one third. *Hardy Varieties of Wheat*

Railroad extension in the Northwest is bewildering. The railway kings are in a helpful war of emulation by which the north country west from the Mississippi to the Rockies is being gridironed, until the map of the Dakotas and Montana resembles in cross lines the eastern states. In North Dakota a main line sends out a dozen laterals into Canada and as many southward. Two other roads branch into as many feeders. Seven main lines now cross the state. Heretofore South Dakota has had no railroads westward from the Missouri River. Now three lines with branches are intersecting it. Fourteen railways operate in Montana. One new line is pushing straight to the Pacific. Most of this traffic will strike Puget Sound. *Railroad Extension*

Electrical Power

Where the railways cross the Rockies there is no pass corresponding to the Columbia opening through the Coast Range; but the roads will utilize the most powerful electrical locomotives known to carry their trains over the mountains. This means increased power and saving of coal, and cars now used for coal liberated for other freight. The water needed for electricity is at hand. The Spokane River with four hundred thousand horse power is thought to be the most accessible in the world. An Idaho stream is being harnessed which may electrify five hundred locomotives able to draw one hundred and sixty miles of cars. Electricity demands not only water-power but copper, and the Almighty has hastened his purpose by planting at Butte on the Montana side of the mountains the greatest copper mines thus far discovered. Out of one hill a mile square comes about one fourth of the world's supply. Capitalists harness titanic forces in a competitive race for the Orient. All records in track-laying are outdistanced by roads pushing through Montana.

Immense Ocean Liners

These transcontinental highways are extending across the Pacific by mammoth ocean liners. Either of two sister steamers belong-

The Giant Northwest

ing to one road will swallow in its cavernous maw five hundred car-loads of freight. A first cargo consisted of seventy Baldwin railway locomotives, one hundred railway cars, ten thousand kegs of wire nails, and a half million dollars' worth of hardware, besides a miscellaneous freightage. Her lists when full mean in addition three thousand passengers. And yet with all these growing stupendous facilities the freight of Puget Sound harbor cannot find sufficient carriage.

The Northwest Is a Giant in Its People

Not only may we note this vast centering of forces marshaled and directed toward the awakening East, but let us glance at the multitudes assembling to perform a behest yet dimly understood by us. *[Divine Behest to be Fulfilled]*

In the Puget Sound region itself we have the oldest Christian civilization in the United States west of the Mississippi. Portland is likened to Philadelphia. Here Lee and Whitman brought the gospel to the Indians and knew not that they answered a cry of Asia's millions. The Nez Percés Indians who came to St. Louis for "The white man's Book" were messengers from a Macedonian world. When *[Christian Movements Drawing Continents to God]* the answering missionaries journeyed painfully across parched plains that now are harvest-fields, when later they were prompted to an urgency more than human in securing colonists and pressing upon the government a boundary line that would not leave out Puget Sound, they were God's forerunners in one of the greatest movements of the race. We now see faintly outlined a purpose which is "purposed in the earth," and we may yet come to know that these men wrought as truly and on a scale as colossal as the Bible characters of apostolic days. They planted and nurtured that Northwest civilization which, take it all in all, is not only the most mature, but possibly the most staple of any facing the Pacific; a golden link in a chain to bind the two continents about the feet of God.

Spokane and Montana Populations

Immediately at the back of these coast people are the multitudes crowding into the Spokane country which God scooped out between the mountain ranges. Spreading out from Spokane, hundreds of square miles are being populated by a race ninety-six per cent. Anglo-Saxon. They come from the middle West, the very flower of its development. They learned there how to deal with virgin nature and bring out her highest traits. This new region that others might not understand they readily interpret, and here they are building an inland empire that in wealth progressiveness, and world-consciousness may surpass any region of the West. Next in line is Montana. While her Protestantism does not exceed in numbers a single denomination in some fourth-class cities, and while one fourth of her inhabitants live within two miles of Butte City court-house, making her population elsewhere more scattered, yet, where in eastern Church life do the same number of Christians map and build for the kingdom on anything like the scale of the few in Montana? Their pastors lead by liberal contributions from slender stipends. They outline a program of humane and educational endeavor as broad as Montana itself.

In the Dakotas where Ward and kindred missionary spirits counted their lives not dear, if they might rear a Christian commonwealth, we find a mingling of European races at their best. The foreigners carried North Dakota for prohibition. The people of that state declare that progress, prohibition, and prosperity go together. They say prohibition secures good citizens and shuts out the undesirable from polit-

Dakota Peoples

ical and social life. Minnesota is not included in our frontier, yet she marshals a host of true-hearted Teutons and Scandinavians who peer over the shoulders of the Dakotas Pacificward and potentially represent what may be lacking in forces massing to carry out a divine behest.

Canada to Share in Asia's Transformation

We may deviate somewhat in noting the providential trend in Canadian affairs, yet, it may help us to see more clearly what seems a unifying of North American peoples and forces in the direction of Asia.

Effect of Northern Climate on Wheat

Wheat excels in quality and quantity the nearer it may be grown to the Arctic Circle. The season is short, but furnishes sunshine from 4 A. M. to 10 P. M. Soft wheat from Washington becomes there hard wheat.

American Farmers Trekking Northward

Five hundred thousand American farmers with five hundred millions of dollars have trekked into the Canadian Northwest. Not one tenth of the hundreds of square miles of rich acres have yet been sown. Their extent and richness challenge credence.

A Continental Outlook Toward the Orient

Her ocean fringe is a primeval forest. For years Canada sought reciprocity privileges with the United States. This would warrant building her railroads southward across the line. We repeatedly refused. She was forced to parallel our great transcontinental lines to the Pacific. Canadians no longer talk annexation. They, with good reason, have a sense of self-sufficiency. Their measureless opening resources now roll Pacificward and float from her own Vancouver harbor to the Orient. God's purpose points to a continental movement toward the Far East.

The Problems of the Northwest Are Gigantic

Instinctively we glance oceanward. Our position at the door of Asia in the Philippines looms prophetic. Hawaii, key to the Pacific, is ours. Thought flies back to the Civil War. A different outcome of that conflict would have precluded our interfering in Cuba and prevented our later advance into the East. <small>The Philippines and Hawaii</small>

Spain, once mistress of the Pacific, drops behind the horizon. Again in thought we follow early explorers. Rivers point northwestward. The Missouri was created to point that way and eventually it becomes a water trail. There is but one goal. It is clear why the eyes of other navigators were holden that they should not enter the Columbia River. An unseen sworded angel seemed guarding its mouth until Gray's little ship crept up the coast. The *May-* <small>Our Destiny Pacificward</small>

flower carried the American Republic; **Gray's** vessel, the *Columbia,* was an ark of covenant; it carried law and life for the Orient and its islands of the sea.

Japan and China Changing

We see Japan, the first modern world power of the East. She colonizes in Korea and sends her sons to America to learn of us. China is awakening. Japanese, trained in America, are her schoolmasters. Her latest history dwarfs prophets' dreams. When she comes up to the standard of Japanese living she will have one hundred and fifty millions that she cannot feed, and they will emigrate. She may be able to protect them on any continent.

India Turning Toward Us

India is now turning her face toward America. She has one hundred millions always hungry and they are beginning to emigrate. We set our faces against the Asiatic at close range; yet the Japanese will come, and by sheer force of dominance and persistency their invading line is stretching along our coast. China, despite our exclusion, doggedly sticks to our Pacific shore, and India, met by American mob and Canadian revolt, begins an invasion of our Northwest, in which high-caste Brahman does coarse manual toil in company with those of lower caste.

The Giant Northwest

Our springs of destiny burst forth from the eternal purpose. They feed currents that carry us not only across the Pacific, but into great waters where we do well to yield the helm to God.

The Eternal Purpose

We have entered the gates of the Old World. Our swelling Oriental commerce must prove a highway for our Christ. The real missionaries who arrive and depart along that route will be the Asiatics who come and observe and live and feel among us and then return again and in their mother tongue tell to the waiting children of the East *what they saw and knew and felt.* This northwest territory, so vast, so packed with varied riches, so girded with highways of trade, so filled with chosen peoples; this giant Northwest with its hands gripping Asia, and its face against the Asiatic; what problems begin to stagger it, what issues strive for mastery! As heroically as Lee and Whitman pioneered and planted our first banner there, as truly do hundreds of consecrated preachers on that frontier advance that standard and leaven that commonwealth with the spirit of Christ, the gospel of God's Fatherhood for the race and every man included in the circle of brotherhood.

A Highway for Christ

Foreign and Home Missions Are One

This witnessing of the Church in our Judea and Samaria carries us to the ends of the earth. Foreign missions and home missions are one.

Spirit of the Modern Frontier Preacher

What is the spirit of this modern frontier preacher and his message to us? What stress is upon him and what is God's call to the Church that he be sustained? How are we meeting that call? In answering these questions we note that

The Northwest Is a Giant in Its Needs

Need in Lumber Camps

We glance first at what is secondary. In Washington, Oregon, and Idaho possibly two hundred thousand men, for the greater part of the year, are in lumber camps. The work is constantly shifting and continues Sundays. Modern logging devices keep every man alert and preoccupied during the daylight hours. The men are responsive to manly, tactful missionary effort.

Cheering the Chaplain

A dozen camps, some separated by twenty miles, may constitute a two week's circuit. The missionary travels on foot. When he knows his work the men are glad to see him. The following is a side-light:[1] "I am sure you would have rejoiced if you had been at Camp Three

---
[1] Quoted from Everett T. Tomlinson.

LUMBER CAMP, RAINIER, OREGON

THE RICHEST HILL ON EARTH, BUTTE, MONTANA

last night when I returned from Camp Nine, three miles distant, where I held meetings in the afternoon. I had promised the boys I would return in the evening to hold a second service. It became dark and the boys said, '—— will not come back.' About six-thirty when I came out on the railroad tracks about a quarter of a mile from the camp, I began to sing. The clerk heard me and rushed into the bunk house and called out, '——is coming, boys!' The boys made a break for the door and stood there listening till I got nearer and then the whole fifty of them broke into 'Three cheers for the chaplain,' and I don't believe even Roosevelt would have been cheered more loudly. After a little rest and the cook and 'cookess' had come in, the evening service was opened by singing 'Throw Out the Life-line,' a song they especially enjoy. I asked the foreman if the roof was good and strong, and he assured me that plenty of hay-wire had been used on the corners, so I told the boys to pull out every stop. After a thirty-minute song service, I spoke on 'Excuses,' from Luke xiv, 18, and not a man left his seat during the service. I have some good reports to make when I see you."

Will Affect the Frontier Settlements

While this is a passing phase of work and not directly one of planting churches, yet these men should receive far greater spiritual attention than now. Numbers of them who have pioneered all the way from New Brunswick, hardy, rugged- and great-hearted, remain in the wake of the camps, clear up the land, and build their cabins. The wife is inured to hardship and helps plant the new home. Generally she is of a type that brings out her husband's better qualities. Thus faithful service in the logging camp may strongly influence the frontier settlement.

Mining Communities

The mining town or camp presents one of the most stubborn factors in frontier church life. Foreigners often predominate. This means a repetition of the alien religious situation in other parts of the United States, but with emphasis, for the mines are worked seven days in the week. The mining companies, with notable exceptions, ignore Sabbath law, and not infrequently their less enlightened laborers ignore all law. The mines may be worked in three shifts of eight hours each. Boardinghouses adopt a corresponding schedule for meals and beds. The miners' shifts are changed each week. This means a rotating congregation of those who attend church. Saloons may never close. Three shifts of bartenders cover the twenty-four hours.

Typical Mining City

In a Montana mining city of eighty-five thousand people, a part of whom are miners, there are over two hundred saloons and five breweries. The saloons of that one city outnumber all the churches in that third largest state of the Union. This is a beautiful, modern city. Its various business enterprises, in stability and appointments, fully equal municipalities of its size, yet last year one boarding-house sheltered twenty college bred men only two of whom attended church. Seven attempts to start a Young Men's Christian Association have failed. Churches pull against heavy odds. Thus the work assumes various phases, ranging all the way from large towns, prosperous, materialistic, indifferent, down to settlements that resemble the city slum.

Smaller Towns and Camps

In the smaller, isolated mining towns, and especially in camps, anything like settled, progressive Church life is about impossible. Often a place is a center of other interests besides mining. It may be a supply town for other mines and also it may border on an agricultural region, affording helpful Church conditions.

Important Work

Probably not more than one twentieth of the work of home mission boards is among the mines. Yet it is important. It demands the best talent of the Church. Young business men of large educational equipment are there in numbers. The following gives an idea of the gospel messenger in an Idaho frontier town where mining and other interests unite.

Foster, the Missionary at Council

"Take our work at Council, Idaho. The P. & I. R. R. went up from Weiser to Council—seventy miles. Council has a little cluster of shacks but is the terminal town. It would of necessity be the supply-point for all the region. It is the gateway to the Seven Devils and the Payette Lakes. We sent in Foster. He was a pioneer, versatile, robust with courage, hope, grace, piety. Out of the rough heterogeneous population made up of prospectors, adventurers, and others he gathered a church.

Reaching Out

"The early work was heroic. It had elements of the frontier which were wild, picturesque, comic, tragic, but the little church grew and housed itself in a meeting-house and parsonage. It reached out with mission work to White Schoolhouse, Upper Valley, Mickey, Indian Valley (which had been organized before), Upper District, Midvale, Meadows, West District, Hornet Creek. No other denominations were operating in the field. It was our work. Foster was bishop of the realm, and our society of trained workmen and women covered the territory and was foster-mother to the whole people.

"Foster, the organizer, hero, pioneer, and messenger of God to do the work of the mother missionary society—a wonderful example of the need, energy, efficiency of the work we are doing—work which makes alive the dead wastes of the mountain and wilderness; work that has no ally, no competitor. The field is our own. To neglect it is to relegate the renewed realm to godlessness and vice. Would God our eastern friends could know the power, opportunity, necessity of our missions in the new fields! *[Dead Wastes]*

"Now the tender pathos. 'Minnie' the gentle, earnest, loving wife of Foster, through exposure in the rude shack where they lived and overworked, and her frail body worn out by the hard service and long rides over the rude trails, grew faint, and sinking, gradually went through the golden gate before her life was half spent. *["Minnie"]*

Tribute to Sacrifice

"We buried her at Christmas time. The little camp and all the realm were in tears. Freighters, ranchmen, prospectors, miners, sheep-herders, saloon men, and magdalens wiped away the fast flowing tears. Sweet, silent tribute to a sacrificing life, giving, serving, and making the world better to the last.

A Holy Benediction

"The little church was nearly built when she entered it the last time and sat for an hour in prayerful thought, her tears flowing freely because she knew she might not see the dedication. There was a tender pathos in her words as she said, 'My people will worship here in prayer and song.' The little city was still on the day we buried her. Even the saloons were closed. Love ruled in all hearts. Tears flowed down cheeks of hardy men. Her death was a holy benediction.

Still Forward

"Foster with his four little girls lived and worked. Broken, weary, but sustained, bearing up and going forward. He said, 'I don't know how to preach since Minnie left me, but the people hold me up and say, "You never preached so well." ' "

Crucial Missionary Conditions

Four Sections

Suppose now we unroll our map. Generally

speaking the Northwest is in four parts. The northern prairie, including North and South Dakota and eastern Montana; the Rocky Mountain section, taking in western Montana and part of Idaho; the inter-mountain country between the Rockies and the Coast Range called the Inland Empire, and which we may term the Spokane country; and lastly the Pacific slope.

Let us outline crucial missionary conditions at this date. Beginning with North and South Dakota trace the Missouri River through both states. West of the Missouri, on account of the discovery of dry farming, also because of railway expansion, the development just now, particularly in South Dakota, is so rapid as to submerge all present home missionary provisions to meet the situation. *Present Conditions— The Dakotas*

The seventy thousand square miles of North Dakota are dotted not only with American homes, but Poles, Russians, Germans, Syrians, Hungarians, Hollanders, Icelanders, and half-breeds are there in numbers. In some sections the foreign contingent amounts to sixty or even eighty per cent. of the settlers. *Foreign Settlers in North Dakota*

The American settlers are pouring in from older sections of the country. Fifteen years *American Settlers* ago the population of North Dakota was one hundred and sixty-five thousand, to-day it is more than three times that and in ten years it will reach a million. This is due to railway development. The western third of the state is being homesteaded so rapidly that there are whole counties of new settlers. One town not on the map eight years ago has fifteen hundred people and it takes six or eight men to help the station agent handle the freight.

Towns and Their Moral Direction

The railways building are obliged to lay out towns every twelve miles. A conservative South Dakota business man estimates that this coming development will outrun that of older parts of his state. "Ninety railway stations are building along nine hundred miles of road. Banks, grain-elevators, hotels, general stores; medical, printing, law, and land offices; business and professional interests of all kinds, are inviting young men from the Atlantic to the Pacific to come to a new land. They come where there are no precedents. They must determine them. What shall they be? The Church must answer that.

South Dakota Largely American

South Dakota, on the whole, presents conditions similar to her sister state, but more intensive and on a larger scale. Its people are mostly American. As early as 1900 South Dakota had four hundred thousand inhabitants, only fourteen thousand of whom could not speak English.

The Indians have begun to hold land in severalty in the great reservations breaking up in the south, but they make up less than five per cent. of the population there. *Indians*

A writer pictures the manner in which people arrive and how they begin life on these Dakota prairies. "Each family was permitted to take, free of railroad charge, ten head of live stock, together with household goods and farming implements. When their train trailed up into the new land the pilgrims were emptied into little towns just springing up, or dropped upon the bare and open prairie, one hundred here, two hundred there. Once a party of two thousand overflowed one village of four hundred people. The few settlers who had arrived before them drove in from many miles around and helped the newcomers as best they could. The freight cars were backed on sidings and used to sleep in until the immigrants could build their own homes. Every dwelling, store, church, and schoolhouse within twenty miles was filled to overflowing with these families. *Stream of Homesteaders*

Absorbed by the Prairies

"Within a week, however, the overflow had vanished from the little towns and the freight cars on the prairie siding lost their lodgers. The immigrants brought their horses and farm wagons with them. As soon as their homestead claims were located and filed, they hauled out lumber to build shacks, or with the help of neighbors made their sod houses. Then the 'homesteader' loaded his family, his household goods, and his farming tools into his wagon, and trailed out across the prairie to his new home. The day after he had put the house to rights he began to break land for the spring sowing of wheat. The prairie seemed fairly to swallow these thousands of settlers and to cry for more."[1]

Tide Flowing Into Montana

This tide is pouring from the Dakotas over the borders into Montana and five hundred thousand cattle last year were driven from the ranges never to return. The cowboy vanishes. In eastern and southern Montana the increase in population for the last two years is thrice as rapid as before.

Securing Corner Lots for Churches

A busy skirmish-line reaches out to the foothills of the Rocky Mountains. An alert missionary pioneers along new railroads and picks

---
[1] Paine, *The Greater America*, 86.

up corner lots for churches, and trusts his board to make good on first payments. Incoming people will care for the balance, and everywhere there are invading multitudes.

Suppose we cross the Rocky Mountains into the Inland Empire, the Spokane country. It stretches three hundred and seventy miles westward and more than two hundred miles north and south. It is so new to settlement that on your map it may appear almost a blank; but three hundred thousand people are already there, and they are but the beginning, for steam and electric lines push everywhere. If we cross the Coast Range to the Pacific slope the inhabitants there so increase that the cities of a state double in four years. *Spokane Country and Pacific Slope*

What is the Church doing to meet this situation? It is so new that she is hardly aware of it. Yet in the field itself signs of advance are unmistakable. The few reapers report large harvests. One board in North Dakota last year dedicated fifteen churches. An association admitted ten churches, and could, with men and money, have organized twice as many more in the same territory. Another denomination in one corner of that state has organized forty churches in five years. There is little duplica- *Efforts to Meet the Needs* tion of forces. Out of one hundred and seventy-one societies of one denomination, one hundred and twenty-five are in communities where there is no other Protestant church of the same tongue.

Outlook of the Workers
What is the outlook of men at the front, missionaries who invest everything? One general missionary in North Dakota says that there are eight whole counties where people are going in by the thousand and where towns are springing up in every direction, and the call is insistent for work to be started at many points. Still, he declares, there is yet to be planted the first English-speaking church of his denomination.

One District
A district superintendent of South Dakota now wrestling with eleven great counties has voluntarily attached four other counties westward, and all because otherwise his Church is making no provision to care for that country. His district, thus enlarged, covers fully a third of the southern part of the state. Speaking of his work he says that in ten years his denomination may have a great following there, but if so it means devoted preachers with devoted money to pay them. He reminds us that little men with little money behind them mean diminutive results.

In Montana there are more than two thousand school districts in which no regular services of any kind are held and four fifths of them are never reached at all by any sort of religious influences. The situation grows more distressing as new districts are forming faster than the religious occupation of the old ones, and this has been going on for ten years. A board representative in charge of Montana, who has been a missionary in Africa, says that he found no greater needs on the Dark Continent than in Montana. In the mountains of Idaho are young people of eighteen who have never heard a sermon.

The Unreached in Montana and Idaho

In the Spokane district a superintendent reports that while fifteen hundred communicants have been added in a single year, yet his Church does not occupy one half the places open to it now, and with the present rapid increase of population, within two years he cannot supply one place in four. A bishop says, fifty new churches could be erected if he had an initial building appropriation of twenty-five thousand dollars.

Openings in the Spokane Region

One in charge of a field in Oregon reports that "Across another mountain range are other great rich valleys rapidly being settled

Hunger for the Gospel in Oregon

and developed, but where there is not one sermon in a year. They are hungry, many of them, for the gospel, but we cannot give them any promise under the existing circumstances. We cannot get sufficient money to rightly develop the fields that we are occupying. What can we do with the Macedonian cries? We can only pray and wait.

Wide-spread Religious Destitution

Throughout Washington and Oregon may be found scores of narrow valleys teeming with people. No one is doing anything for them religiously, as but little is attempted by any Church for Washington or Oregon outside the towns. In southwestern Oregon is a county of about fifteen hundred square miles in which live at least twenty-five hundred people, mostly American, and no denomination, according to the report made last year, is doing any work whatever in that whole county. They are absolutely without Church privileges.

Conditions in Western Washington

One in charge of a large field in western Washington does not attempt to enumerate fields that should be occupied this coming year. He declares the religious destitution of western Washington to be appalling; that outside the larger towns very little religious work is being done by any denomination. In his division only two hundred and nine towns out of eleven hundred and forty-six have church organizations *leaving nine hundred and thirty-seven towns and villages without any religious privileges whatever.* Over half the children in western Washington have never been enrolled in a Sunday-school. The whole region is in its infancy and is developing with astounding rapidity. Where in this race is the Church of God?

Self-sacrificing Pastors

You ask what about these missionary pastors? The circuit system is their only possible method. One preacher, for example, has a parish ten miles wide and forty miles long. In it are four towns aggregating twelve hundred people in addition to wide reaches of rural communities. He drives thirty miles each Sunday, preaches three times and holds services on week-nights. He is the only pastor of any kind officiating in that field, yet adjoining unshepherded communities of fifty and a hundred people desire a sermon from him if only now and then. This, of course, is impossible. People in these wide parishes, in attending worship make sacrifices we know nothing about. They travel ten and twenty miles and return.

Far-stretching Circuits

Difficulties of Travel

The missionaries in Idaho must travel many miles on foot, because at times of the year neither horse nor conveyance can follow the road. Snow-shoes are seen at the doorway of the missionary. Streams and mountain torrents must be forded. One of them writes, "Mud, slush, miles, leagues, mountains, streams unbridged, forests not tenanted, canyons unlighted, wolves unmuzzled, and other things too numerous to mention are more interesting than attractive, along some of the ways to the places where the people are to be found."

Slender Support

These men, all too few, whom the Church sends into these wide fields, she slenderly supports. The cost of living is high. Out of a salary of say six hundred dollars must be paid a fuel bill of one hundred dollars. The preacher may keep two horses to cover his wide stretch of country. How are we allowing families of our missionary preachers to live? If it were not for the opportune supplies of Woman's Home Missionary organizations, man after man would have been literally starved off the field. Heroines live in those parsonages.

Unwavering Courage

And how do these men feel? Are they ready to retreat? One in referring to the present speaks for himself. "The marks of stress and strain are everywhere apparent when we look over this year of financial famine; for in it we have lived on half rations, with one half the appropriation of five years ago and a larger camp to care for than we had then. And yet, with the exception of two or three fields that, because of a lack of appreciation of our situation, considered themselves unjustly discriminated against, not a murmur has been voiced. Hardships have been borne and posts have been maintained with grim determination and cheerful hope, and wherever there came a chance for a dash into new territory the response has been no sullen protest that we have more than we can take care of, but a cheer and a rush that have put new life into our ranks. So even if our faces are a little drawn and belts pulled up a hole or two more than normal we come out of the year with the unfailing good humor and optimism of the American, with some new gains to record, and a discipline that has done us good.

"Do you wonder that we do not more rapidly reach self-support in these vast stretches of country, where our churches are scores and often hundreds of miles apart? Do you won-

Call for Christian Coöperation

der that reductions seriously cripple us; that we are in desperate need of funds; that every cut on the scant allowance made for so great and so growing a state means the cutting down of life necessities; that it means pruning the tree down to the root-stock with little chance for leafage and none for fruit? Never has our nation watched a development so rapid in any section of her domain. Never were opportunities for so colossal a worldwide influence spread before men as are now spread out on this Pacific coast. Never were calls for Christian help more numerous and urgent. And never have our hands been so fettered and our resources so limited. We do not urge more equitable distribution, but juster appreciation. We do not ask that Massachusetts should have less but that the great West should have more. We do not ask you to cut off slices from other states that we may eat, but we do plead for such increased giving to our national Society as will allow a proportionate generous provision for us. Invest in us. We will pay it back. Grub-stake us, brethren; your share will be enormous. Advance the capital for locations and prospects and operating expenses, and you will see astonishing returns."

The Giant Northwest

Our Responsibility

We are trustees of a giant heritage. Lee and Whitman and a consecrated host bought it with their lives. What is our sacrifice? Our Northwest and its Puget Sound country face the Orient. Are we making it a world base of supply? We feed Asia with wheat, what about the bread of life? A farmer in Illinois, who gets his mail by rural free delivery, sent a hundred dollars to one of the home missionary boards. He said the offering meant pinching and saving for his wife and self, as the net income of their little farm was less than three hundred dollars. Before this he had sent liberal checks to the same board. He writes that there are so many opportunities to help the Master, he is going to do his best for a little while yet. He quotes a modern preacher that "Heaven lies just beyond where a fellow does his best." Is not his life so linked to God's world purpose that he plows as well as prays unto the Lord? His zeal exemplifies the spirit that will animate the Church.

<small>*Trustees of a Precious Heritage*</small>

> "The weary ones had rest, the sad had joy
>   That day, and wondered how.
> A ploughman *singing* at his work had prayed,
>   'Lord, help them now.'"

QUESTIONS ON CHAPTER III

AIM: TO SHOW THE MARVELOUS MATERIAL PROGRESS AND POSSIBILITIES AND THE RELIGIOUS NEEDS OF THE NORTHWEST

1. Name the states that are included in the Northwest.
2. How did these states become a part of the United States?
3. Compare them in area with New York, Pennsylvania, Iowa, and Georgia.
4. Compare the Northwest in area with Germany, France, and England.
5. What other state can be added to Ohio and Pennsylvania to equal the area of Oregon?
6. Locate the Northwest in latitude with countries in Europe and Asia.
7. Can you name any inlet in the United States that offers greater natural harbor facilities than Puget Sound?
8. How much nearer is Puget Sound to China and Japan than San Francisco?
9. Name some of the principal products of the Northwest that the Orient needs.
10.* Will the Panama Canal stimulate trade between the East and West coasts of the United States?
11. Name some of the products of the Northwest that are needed in the East.
12. Compare the climate in Oregon and Montana with that in the state where you live. Which do you prefer, and why?

13.* As a young man where would you prefer to establish yourself in business, in the East or the Northwest? Give reasons.
14.* Name some of the difficulties in Christian work among lumbermen?
15. Name some of the temptations peculiar to lumbermen and miners.
16. What two extremes in social and intellectual life are found among miners?
17.* Name some of the difficulties in Christian work among miners.
18.* Among which one of these two classes would you prefer to work, and why?
19. How does the inrush of foreigners magnify the home mission problem in the Northwest?
20.* Name some of the difficulties in Christian work among homesteaders.
21. Why cannot they support a minister and build their own church?
22. Did the church with which you are connected receive any financial assistance outside of the local community when it was first organized?
23.* Describe what you would consider an ideal minister in one of these Northwestern parishes.
24. Where would you find such a man now?
25. How large should his salary be?
26.* If Christianity is not strongly entrenched in our country can we hope to win the Orient for Christ?
27.* Give as many reasons as you can why you believe that the Church should immediately increase its force of Christian workers in the Northwest.

REFERENCES FOR FURTHER STUDY
CHAPTER III

I. *The Northwest.*
   Carr: "The Great Northwest." Outlook, June, '07.
   Clark: Leavening the Nation, XIII.
   Northrop: "The Great Northwest." World To-day, January, '06.
   Oberholtzer: "Opening of the Great Northwest." Century, March, '07.
   Rader: in Methodism and the Republic, 63-78.
   Puddefoot: The Minute Man on the Frontier, X.

II. *Oregon.*
   Clark: Leavening the Nation, XIII.
   Drake: The Making of the Great West, 233-241.
   Elford: "Oregon; An Inland Empire." Overland Monthly, June, '05.
   Van Dyke: "Big Woods of Oregon." Outing, February, '06.

III. *Washington.*
   Clark: Leavening the Nation, XIII.

IV. *Montana.*
   Clark: Leavening the Nation, X.
   Elrod: "Resources of Montana and Their Development." Science, May 20, '04.

V. *Marcus Whitman.*[1]
   Mowry: Marcus Whitman, XII.
   Nixon: How Marcus Whitman Saved Oregon, VI, VIII, X.
   Shelton: Heroes of the Cross in America, IV.

---
[1] For additional references, see Bibliography, pages 265-279. Reference should also be made to denominational missionaries who pioneered in these sections.

THE WEST BETWEEN AND BEYOND

Below the Grand Canon of the Colorado, with Nevada and California on the west and Arizona on the east, is a region of great aridity. Here date-palms, oranges, lemons, pomegranates, figs, sugar, and cotton flourish where water can be applied, and ultimately a region of country can be irrigated larger than was ever cultivated along the Nile, and all the products of Egypt will flourish therein.
—*Powell*

Nevada farmers are very prosperous on the average, taking one year with another, and probably much more so than the farmers in more pretentious localities. For the most part, they were poor when they came and have grown steadily better off. The climate is perfectly adapted to the production of all the cereals and hardy fruits. The wheat is perfect, with a full, rich kernel and a clean, golden straw, free from smut and rust. It has taken prizes at all the great expositions. With a variety of soil, on the different slopes of hillside, plain, and valley, there are conditions to meet almost every requirement in an agricultural way within the limitations of climate.

The great industry of Wyoming from the time of its first settlement has been stock-raising. Its agriculture has been mostly auxiliary to this. Herds of horses, cattle, and sheep are grazed upon the enormous free pasture or range from spring to autumn, and then fed upon the native or alfalfa hay raised in the irrigated valleys. This industry has been the source of local prosperity and enlisted great sums of eastern and foreign capital.
—*Smythe*

IV

THE WEST BETWEEN AND BEYOND[1]

Outstanding Features

San Francisco harbor, possibly not less important than Puget Sound in the Northwest, is the Pacific golden gateway opening from this marvelous young domain toward an ancient hemisphere. Kansas City is a railway portal from the east, guarding the entrance to both this west and the southwest country. A study of a good railway map is suggestive. It marks the zones of development and shows radiating centers. The railways dominate the West. Wherever they pass through regions with possibilities towns and settlements string the line like beads. A relief map is expressive. Nebraska and Kansas gradually rise westward. Wyoming and Colorado are like a high rolling sea solidified. The Rocky Mountains strike straight down through these states. The climax is Colorado, the highest state between the

---
[1] The section that lies between the Northwest and the Southwest: Western Kansas, Western Nebraska, Colorado, Wyoming, Utah, Southern Idaho, Nevada, and parts of California.

oceans. It is a continental watershed. Next, between the Rockies and the Coast Range, are Utah, southern Idaho, and Nevada, a high broken table-land, yet, by contrast to the regions rimming them, they form a mammoth inland basin. Then follows a precipitous plunge over the Sierras, which lands us in semi-tropical California.

Great Variety These altitudes and valleys, wind-swept plains and sheltered lowlands, afford a variety of climate, productiveness, and scenery nowhere duplicated in an equal area. They probably embrace the richest mining belt on the planet. Colorado towers not only physically above this "West Between" domain, but, apart from California, in development it is easily the most advanced state therein. Wyoming is comparatively crude. Utah is one-sided in both material and moral growth. Nevada is a lusty infant. All are big with treasure and unfolding strength, but in Colorado, while all is morning, there is ripeness and maturity of life. In Colorado, Wyoming, Idaho, and Utah, woman enjoys the right of suffrage equally with man.

Self-evident Need In the western parts of Nebraska and Kansas we have missionary conditions less intensive, but similar to those in North and South Dakota, described in the last chapter. New railway development, dry farming, and irrigation are in evidence. It will be hard to convince any missionary of these wide fields that the Northwest offers conditions more critical or places more numerous that should instantly receive the open-handed consideration of the Church.

Colorado

A glance at the map might leave an impression that Colorado is about two thirds uninhabitable mountains: but these ranges are scarred by many narrow valleys with a climate all their own. Colorado's western slope presents a marked contrast to its eastern half. Warm winds from the Gulf of California make localities there ideal for luscious fruits. "Peach Day" at Grand Junction means free bounty to all who come. On this west slope there is more water than irrigable land. Eastern Colorado was first developed. It began with the railway. Capital was munificent. Streams of immigrants coöperated and the new commonwealth leaped forward amazingly. First was the gold mining which now pays fifty millions of dollars a year; also two millions of irrigated acres con-

Immense Resources of Colorado

tribute forty millions, manufactures one hundred million dollars, and other added sources equal manufactures. This is all within one generation. Colorado has a population of more than half a million. Its climate and scenery are famous.

Public-spirited Men

This state has been fortunate in its public-spirited men. Immense fortunes taken from mines and various enterprises have been expended in the commonwealth that bestowed them. This is in marked contrast to the spirit of capitalists who in the past have exploited Nevada and Wyoming, and spent elsewhere the millions extracted there. Thus Denver ranks as one of the most beautiful and progressive cities of the Union. Colorado Springs, by the public spirit of a leading citizen, has become nationally noted as a place of residence. The Greeley Colony, founded on irrigation, has been a model for other like laudable settlements.

Elements of Progress

Twenty-four railways penetrate all parts of the state. Zealous local pride and patriotism make available the people's best for Colorado's uplift. Its religious and intellectual life is vigorous. Its churches, at the centers, are strong. Its public and Church schools are excellent.

The West Between and Beyond 121

Missionary opportunities, however, are numerous and striking.

It is difficult for people in older sections to understand why a wealthy young state should not fully care for its own religious interests. If the Church, in such states, controlled the wealth there the case would be reversed. In the growth of a commonwealth, however, among its latest developments is the devotement of large treasure to Jesus Christ. Rapid material progress at the start instils a materialism that makes outside contributions to spiritual ends even the more necessary. But such missionary beginnings will prove fruitful.

Outside Contributions Still Required

The first Protestant denomination in Colorado began in Central City. Last year that particular congregation gave an average of three dollars per member for missions. Nevertheless, the general situation is so new that a single denominational body says of one part of the state: "If we had the money we could this year build twenty-five new churches and open forty-two new preaching places." Many localities have never had a minister. People will come pouring into the state as a result of present railway extension. The returns on present Church investments will be great. One

Large and Quick Returns Possible

denomination increased by three thousand members last year, about three times the rate of the year before. One superintendent asks help to open fifteen places. Another declares: "If I had three hundred dollars I could put five preachers into five counties where there is no Protestant service held, and a multitude of people making new homes are there asking us to come to them."

Pressure on Scattered Workers

A similar story comes from many quarters. The pressure on isolated workers is tremendous. A missionary writes that they cannot press the battle to the utmost. The thin line of attack is so painfully scattered that there is no shoulder to shoulder courage in the conflict.

An Extensive Circuit

In Baca County one pastor has a circuit covering two hundred miles which must be traveled by team. His salary is four hundred dollars. He reports forty conversions for the year. He invests his life. How much does it cost us? "We can take much out of the life of a circuit preacher and his family, but we cannot get it all that way."

Urgent Appeals

From fifty to a hundred thousand people came into eastern Colorado last year. One writes: "Appeal after appeal comes to me from this great area [Colorado and adjacent states]. Shall we falter now or shall we furnish the sinews of war for those who are willing to make the heroic sacrifices and go for their Master's and these people's sakes"?

Wyoming

Wyoming, with physical features less pronounced than Colorado, is a marked contrast in internal improvement. It has probably not far from one hundred and twenty-five thousand people, less than one and a half per square mile, for a territory about twice the size of New York State. It has immense untouched mineral and other natural resources. Fully one fifth of the state is underlaid with coal. Its petroleum has named it the "Pennsylvania of the West."

Wyoming, the Pennsylvania of the West

A million acres are irrigated or in process of reclamation. Its irrigation law is widely known and has been extensively copied. It is based on the proposition that water belongs to the public. About one ninth of the state is covered with forests. Hundreds of manufactures are in operation. It is, however, preeminently a grazing country. In a single year its wool clip was six millions of dollars. Its cattle number seven hundred thousand. Lack of railways has

Grazing and Irrigation

prevented progress. Only one line has traversed the state, and that through the most uninviting part. After years of slow advance a resident missionary says concerning the new situation: "Happily, now all this has changed. On all sides the doors have not only been opened, but have been torn off their hinges to admit the homesteader. The national government seems to vie with the state government in paving the way for the settlement of this commonwealth. The discovery that this is one of the richest states in the Union in natural resources has been followed by the order for the expenditure of millions of dollars in irrigation projects. All this without a dollar of cost, other than the actual expense per acre, accrues to the purchaser. For the land he pays fifty cents per acre; for the water right he pays in ten equal payments, running over ten years, just what it costs. With ten millions of arable acres subject to settlement on these or other easy terms, it seems needless for anybody to remain land hungry.

Railway Lines and Mineral Deposits

"These conditions are bringing thousands of excellent farmers from Iowa, Illinois, Indiana, Missouri, Nebraska, and elsewhere. Not a desolate waste, but a 'land of milk and honey,' this is found to be. Instead of a country where blizzards breed, it is in many respects the best climate on the continent. The railroads, too, are contributing to the development of the state. Instead of a single railway along the southern border there are soon to be four roads intersecting the state from east to west. Two other lines are to cross the state from north to south. Deposits of coal, iron, copper, lead, silver, and gold are attracting investors from every quarter."

This superintendent adds that conditions now call for twice the present pastoral force in his field. His denomination had less than four hundred members in that state ten years ago, now they have more than four times that number, and about twenty-two hundred in Sunday-schools. Yet, at best, many live pitiably isolated from a gospel ministry. We quote from a missionary periodical: "Back from the railroads are hundreds of homes and ranches, forty to one hundred and fifty miles from the town where the people go once or twice a year to do their trading, camping out while going and coming. They do not mind these things in health, but when sickness and death come, God be merciful!

Call for Mission Re-enforcement

Lonely Sorrow

"Some time ago death entered a home that was one hundred and twenty miles from the railroad and took away a little child. No people outside the family were there at the time and a furious blizzard raged without. It was necessary that some one should ride that one hundred and twenty miles to the town. There was no one to go but the mother's sister, a young girl, so she threw the saddle on her pony and started at midnight for the destination which she reached the next day. Here a little casket and some clothing was strapped on the back of the saddle and on the evening of the third day the girl arrived at the stricken home having ridden two hundred and forty miles. At that sad burial there was no one in that whole countryside to offer a prayer, read a passage of Scripture, or speak a word of comfort to those who were in sorrow.

Years of Waiting

"A missionary went into that country later on, and one of the old-timers grasped his hand and looking wistfully into his face said: 'Sir, we have waited twenty years for you.' Why was this? Not because the missionary societies were not doing their part, but because the churches had allowed the missionary treasuries to become empty.

"One of our missionaries took a territory twenty thousand square miles in extent in which there were seven churches and eight missions, with nine new ones to open. In that whole territory there were but half a dozen churches of other denominations and they, for the most part, were pastorless. Twenty thousand square miles! What could one or two or three ministers do? And one day when the missionary was two hundred miles down the road a little procession wound its way through a gap in the mountain. There were cowboys booted and spurred, some weeping women, and in an old wagon a long pine box. The little company stopped at the edge of a little hamlet, and one of the boys rode up to the general store and asked the manager if there was a gospel slinger there? The manager, a deacon in our little church, shook his head; he could not tell those people that the missionary society could not help support a missionary and they were without a pastor. The cowboy's head dropped, and he seemed overcome by his disappointment. 'We thought sure there'd be some one here. Bill's bronc stepped in a gopher hole day 'fore yesterday and throwed and dragged him. We——kind'r—thought——'

The Pathetic Quest

A Layman's Response

"The manager looked across that burning waste to that pathetic little group waiting so patiently. He choked up, then told the man to call his friends and go to the church, and himself, his fright forgotten in his sympathy, conducted the services."

Keep Watch of Wyoming

The Church which keeps in touch with Wyoming for the next few years and shows its faith by generous reenforcements of money and workers, will raise up for itself and the kingdom a mighty following. Keep close watch of the map of Wyoming.

Great Interior Basin

Depressed Area

Utah, Nevada, and southern Idaho are parts of our "Great Interior Basin." Each continent of the world has a similar depression. That of Europe is the largest, ours is the smallest. It has been known as the "Great American Desert." Its waters do not get beyond its borders. The rivers all flow into lakes that have no outlets or they are lost in desert sands. It embraces the southeastern part of Oregon, parts of Idaho and Wyoming, the whole of Nevada, about half of Utah, a strip off the eastern line of California, and a large area in the southern part of that state.

The West Between and Beyond

Dimensions and Elevation

It has a roughly triangular shape with its apex to the south. Each angle is occupied by extensive irrigated areas or irrigation projects. Its extreme length is eight hundred and eighty miles and its width at the latitude of Salt Lake City about five hundred and seventy-two miles. Its area approximates two hundred and ten thousand square miles. At its widest point the general elevation of the lowlands is three thousand feet. A central elevated region north and south divides the desert into two areas of relative depressions with Salt Lake, Utah, on the east and Carson, Nevada, on the west.

Broadly Sketched

"Southward the land descends to even below sea-level in the Imperial Valley. The rivers all flow into lakes that have no outlet or are lost in desert sands. In the eastern depression, the Mormons since 1847 have partially developed the territory by irrigation. In Carson basin, Nevada, about ninety thousand acres are under cultivation by private enterprise and there is enough other land susceptible of irrigation, because of the water-supply, to bring the total up to five hundred and fifty thousand acres. The Truckee-Carson irrigation scheme built by the government will reclaim nearly four hundred thousand acres.

Irrigation Possibilities

"Nevada is the dryest arid state. It is the most thinly populated of any in the Union, having only about fifty thousand people. Its area, 109,140 square miles, is equal to that of Italy, which has a population seven hundred and fifty times as great. Not one of its acres in a hundred is improved farm land, thus it has more territory for settlers than any other part of the United States. The irrigated area in Utah comprises eight counties and has about two hundred thousand inhabitants. Nevada on its acres that may be irrigated, and are already under cultivation, will support at least half a million. Mines decrease in value but irrigated lands are an endless source of revenue. Several railways cross this Great Basin. In building these lines skeletons of those who perished in the old emigrant days were exhumed. It was then clearly revealed that in several places the grave-diggers were actually within a few feet of good water which to them would have proved a priceless boon, for beneath those burning sands water is found all over the basin, pure and sweet, at the depth of from eight to twenty feet. These lands, when watered, are of amazing fertility."[1]

[1] C. J. Blanchard.

From Stereograph, copyright, 1901, by Underwood & Underwood, New York
THE PRIDE OF THE MORMONS—THE TEMPLE, SALT LAKE CITY, UTAH

Utah and Mormonism

Utah requires study. It is "a succession of mountains, desert valleys, and crystal streams, and scattered over it all is the wealth of the mine and the sleeping potentiality—here and there partially awakened—of the home, the field, the orchard, and the workshop." *A Glance at Utah*

The largest portion of the population, two hundred and fifty thousand, live in a section covered by a two hours' railway ride from Provo to Ogden. The agriculture of Utah is more diversified and hence more completely self-sustaining than that of any other western state. More than five hundred thousand acres are irrigated and twice as much more will soon be added. This is a field affording large and favorable opportunities for growth in population, and the territory available is well scattered over the state. *Present and Future Population*

The Mormons in Utah and elsewhere number probably about two hundred and fifty thousand. They have some twenty-three hundred missionaries. They aim ultimately to have two missionaries in every county of the United States. An element of perpetuity is that, in the eyes of the law, the children of polygamous *Position of Mormonism* marriages are illegitimate. This fact, in proportion as the young people become educated, tends to an adherence to Mormonism and its teachings for self-defense. Most people have too much sense to accept Mormon teachings if, at the beginning, the Mormon missionaries explained the system as they do later to those who become identified with their communities. By that time the person finds himself so involved that it is not convenient to retract. Mormonism is un-American. It is squarely opposed to the national government as such, counts itself *the* government and submits to the laws of the United States only when it becomes impossible to resist. Even in these days a polygamist, self-confessed, is elected to Congress and not unseated by the United States government. Thus Mormonism seems influential out of all proportion to its numbers.

Monstrous Religious Teachings

The religious teachings of the Mormons concerning God and human life are vile and monstrous. Unless one be confronted with the evidence, his imagination will hardly mount to the absurdities of this sect.

Aggressiveness

Nothing is more opposed to Christianity. It aims to control the politics of the state. It now has the balance of power in Idaho, Utah, and

The West Between and Beyond 133

Wyoming. It is making headway in that direction in Montana, Colorado, and Nevada. The Mormons are pioneers in the cultivation of irrigated land. They push into the newly reclaimed sections. The Church must be alert and aggressive or it will find that the irrigated districts of several states have become centers so dominated by Mormon influence that the gospel may be greatly hindered as an influence leavening the new communities.

A Mission Field

The Mormons have opposed the education of the common people. Missionary schools helped to force them into an educational system. Then more than one half of six hundred public schools were utilized to propagate Mormon teachings. Publicity ended this. They are forced to higher standards intellectually and are framing a philosophy of Mormonism. Thus unwillingly, but irresistibly, Mormonism is being pushed into the light. This is a great advance for truth, and places them on the defensive. The increase of Gentile immigration and the rising intelligence among its own young people are a serious menace to this foe. Reports of missionaries show a goodly list of

(margin note: Leaven of Schools and Truth)

Mormons who have been won by the direct preaching of the gospel.

Meeting Real Needs

The denominations which for years have been laying deep educational foundations are those now reaping the larger harvests. The wife of an influential Mormon remarked that she dislikes sending her children to a certain Protestant mission school. She knew that the local missionary leader of that denomination opposed her husband, but, she said, she could not do otherwise, as that school was the best.

Strength of the System

Mormon leaders urge their young people to prepare themselves for their destiny, which is to hold the reins of the United States government. We must maintain mission schools and the gospel that the young of Utah may learn patriotism. Many of the Mormon people are worthy of our sympathy. They have, for the most part, been recruited out of the sturdy ignorant class, from parts of Europe and this country, and numbers of them would doubtless never have identified themselves with Mormonism had they known what they later learned. The difficulties attending upon renouncing Mormonism and separation from it are great. Converts to Christianity there may find it necessary to remove to other communities in order to escape the evils of a virtual boycott. Master organization reaches to the last individual and any signs of indifference call for immediate attention.

For a woman, once a Mormon, to turn her back upon it means heroism of the highest order. If the Church, by any adequate measures, will meet the Mormon situation with a tithe of the sacrifice and determination that repentant Mormons must exercise to become Christians, the outlook will become far different than at present. We have no home field with a record for sustained and heroic missionary service surpassing that of Utah. Men who for many years have been doing Christian work there consider it the hardest field either home or foreign. Only the most consecrated type of workers will succeed. A general missionary says: "It is hard to get good men to come to Utah. After coming most of them leave at the first disappointment. *We need men here with the same settled conviction that takes others to the foreign field. A conviction that God has called them to this as a life-work.* A pastor worked in a town ninety-seven per cent. Mormon for twelve years and in the last year has baptized more converts than during all the pre-

A Peculiarly Hard Field

ceding years. Suppose he had left two years ago?"

Signs of Encouragement

A sign of encouragement is the political revolt in Salt Lake City. The Smoot case enkindled great fear among the Mormons. Railway magnates are securing the Salt Lake City electric light and railway system, and are building new lines. Millions of dollars are being spent there on railway terminals. Several of the largest smelters in the world are going up. The mining output for 1906 was one third greater than any preceding year. A Gentile in Salt Lake City is investing millions of dollars in improved real estate. The new railroads and government irrigation schemes are opening new towns. As the Gentiles move in the Mormons may find it increasingly difficult to retain their control as heretofore. One denomination reports that in its membership in Utah ten per cent. has come from Mormon families.

Must be Adequate Investment

We can never succeed in Utah save by expensive methods. We must strongly reenforce the boards working there. Present provision is inadequate. This kind goeth not out but by extraction. Enough has been accomplished to show that the investment is well worth making now.

The West Between and Beyond 137

Gratitude of a Convert

How the gospel appears to a converted Mormon may be somewhat understood from the following written by one who is now a consecrated missionary teacher: "If there was any one thing that convinced me more than another that Mormonism is not true, it was in comparing the lives of the mission teachers with the lives of the Mormons. I hear much about the work in Utah being discouraging. There may be cause for being discouraged, yet I doubt whether there is a mission field in Utah where there have not been seen conversions. Am I selfish? I may be, yet I cannot help feeling that the salvation of my soul was worth all the money spent at ———— and the sacrifices of the missionaries when I consider what I have been saved from—Mormonism with all its satanic teachings and practises." This emphasizes the point that the Church which maintains the best schools in Utah will contribute most to the overthrow of Mormonism.

Stronger Support

"The question may be asked why Protestant forces have not accomplished more all these years. What sort of a chance have we given them? How have they been backed up? Is it not a wonder that more workers have not died of loneliness? They have been so few and their equipment has been so meager. Results in proportion to investment have not been wanting. It is high time for the Church to awake to its own neglect. It may be found at last that misguided Mormons may form but a small minority as against those in the Church of God who have extended no hand and have helped open no way for their escape."

Idaho

Mormons in Idaho

In swinging northward from Utah into southern Idaho we are still in the Great Basin and in a Mormon region. About half of the six thousand in Pocatello are Mormons. They have there a twenty thousand dollar church. This proportion of Mormons holds in other large towns of southeastern Idaho, while in the agricultural district the ratio reaches eighty or ninety per cent.

Examples of Success

Yet throughout the state Protestantism is winning. At Twin Falls a church started four years ago is now building a thirty thousand dollar structure. An enterprising missionary rented a room at Weiser. The outlook was discouraging. He found twelve members the first day. In eight days he had built a temporary structure costing a hundred and fifty dollars. A revival followed and in a month the membership grew to forty-five. They now have one hundred and fifty members and a six thousand dollar building.

Nevada

Nevada is the fourth state in size in the Union. Its southern boundary is in the same latitude as South Carolina while its northern limit is on a line with Massachusetts. In the Carson Valley or sink we have the depression corresponding to the Salt Lake Valley on the other side of the Great Basin. Nevada is a vast table-land averaging in altitude about four thousand feet. Its new development is, if possible, more sensational than that of other western states. *Giant Nevada*

While there are new mining interests which may surpass any of the past, yet the present and the future larger prosperity of Nevada is based on agriculture. The agricultural output over a series of years will not only eclipse the wealth from the mines, but in an especial sense it will tend to the more rapid development of that state. The farmers will find a ready market at the mining towns for all they can produce and at good prices. The mining town will *Outlook for Agriculture* be greatly benefited thereby, because good living supplies will be at hand in abundance instead of those now shipped from a distance and sold at exorbitant rates.

Lines of Rapid Growth

The Truckee-Carson irrigation project in the Carson sink and Goldfield mine discoveries are the two chief factors in recent rapid increase in population. About sixteen hundred miles of new railway were built in 1907. The Goldfield population leaped last year to eighteen thousand and seven millions of dollars are being spent on new buildings and improvements. Three other towns with an aggregate of twelve thousand are near. In eastern Nevada, Ely, the great copper-mining city, promises to be the Butte of Nevada. Its population trebled in five years.

Threshold of a New Era for the Church

The Churches have a great field in this state. They are entering into its life. The mines are now largely owned and managed by men who are building homes in the state. Dividends are being invested there. The needs are greater than ever and the situation demands money and men at once. At Reno, the capital, there are students who, until they entered the state university, never had the opportunity of attending a church service or Sunday-school. "Nevada to-day offers a magnificent opportunity to the

TRUCKEE-CARSON PROJECT, NEVADA
PURE-BLOODED APACHE LABORERS CONSTRUCTING A ROAD THROUGH THE DESERT

The West Between and Beyond 141

Christian missionary. It has generous, willing men and women who will repay a thousand fold any real interest taken in the spiritual welfare of the state. The only question is who will come and come at once."

A missionary superintendent with a territory about seven hundred and fifty miles square, traveled during the year fifteen thousand miles. One mile in seven was by private conveyance. Living expenses are high. He cites an extreme case of hay selling at ninety dollars per ton and wood at eighty-five dollars per cord. This is a part of his statement to his general committee: {*Expansive Figures*}

"We have our banner unfurled in ninety-eight different communities that I know of, and are giving the people some sort of religious service. In a number of cases this amounts only to a Sunday-school or an occasional visit of a minister, but it is all that the people can support at this time. {*Brave Beginnings*}

"This territory which is the arena of our conflict is receiving more than a passing notice from the world about us. The prophecy of my predecessor made years ago, and reiterated from time to time, is wondrously coming to pass: 'The new and greater Nevada is upon us.' The tide ebbed until the mud flats were {*Greater Nevada at the Door*} bare but it is flowing in upon us again covering all former marks, obliterating for us the rocks and sands of former shores and making new Golden Gates and sunny harbors.

Magic of the Waters

"We have one of the greatest farming countries in America. We have the soil; we have always had it. The problem of the West has always been not one of soil but water for the soil. In the great basin of the Lower Carson Uncle Sam has opened his great nine million dollar farm, on which he has undertaken to deliver the water to 4,375 homesteads of eighty acres each. And he has made good. The water is flowing over the land in great abundance. And this is only a beginning. Similar schemes on the part of the government will take hold, not only of the waters of the Truckee, but doubtless also of the Humboldt, the Walker, the Carson, as well as other streams. Private capital is already interested in the reclamation of swamp and desert land in Fall River, Honey Lake, Carson, Antelope, Smith, Humboldt, and Owen River valleys, opening up these great rich valleys to thousands of home seekers. The new Nevada is upon us, and it is not a desert Nevada. It is a Nevada of green fields, of alfalfa, and of waving grain, of great fruit orchards, of spring-time flowers, and singing birds.

"Nevada is also the center of activity along the line of railroad building. Recently there have been opened up in the Tonopah and Goldfield, the Las Vegas and Tonopah, the Goldfield and Bullfrog, the Nevada Northern, the Sante Fé to Searchlight, the Fallon branch of the Southern Pacific, and the Virginia and Truckee branch to Gardenerville. In addition to this the great Western Pacific transcontinental line crosses our entire territory. Great railroad corporations, to the extent of millions of money, believe in the future of Nevada. Thousands of men with all sorts of businesses are coming to us, seeing their opportunity. An investment to-day means large returns to-morrow. Institutions of all kinds move with speed and power.

Railroad Activity

"The only institution that seems, comparatively speaking, to be 'marking time' is the Church of Jesus Christ. Why is it? I do not know a single religious denomination that, from my view-point at least, is doing one half of the work it might accomplish. When every other sort of business concern sees its opportunity, why does the greatest business

The Church Must Awake

corporation known to man neglect its opportunity? In writing for publication and in personal letters and conversations not a few, and repeatedly from the platform, I have said that 'Dollars invested by our Church to-day, in propagating work in Nevada, will return in thousands to-morrow.' But the question of money return ought to have no part in the problem. The people *are here* and *are coming to us by the thousands.* Jesus died on Calvary to save them. The Church has a duty to perform concerning their salvation."

California

Western California

In northern California is a retarded expansion caused by large sections of country held heretofore for grazing and raising grain. The coming development of inland waterways there and also the quickening of the soil by moisture are presenting the Church with conditions sure to become acute unless intelligently considered. One who travels over that country tells his board that he has work as purely missionary as can be found anywhere in the United States.

San Francisco a Center of Power

It is difficult to appreciate the sweep of power emanating from San Francisco. No city or state of the Union, exclusive of itself, holds

The West Between and Beyond 145

anything like the grip of this metropolis on the Oriental world. We have pictured Puget Sound and shown its pregnant relationship to the East. San Francisco is differently situated commercially, yet holds overbalancing present-day advantages. It is central on the coast, with no frontier inconveniently near. Much of the territory covered by this chapter is tributary to it. Lines of influence, like sun's rays, radiate from and center there from every part of the United States. As a financial hub where converge world forces it also radiates across the Pacific. It is full-orbed. In it cluster the greatest Christian Oriental propagandas on this side of the globe. From America nothing religiously affects China and Japan so profoundly as the work of home mission boards in San Francisco. Church schools there are international. One great denomination grips Japan from San Francisco almost as effectively as by its agencies in that country.

This is a large subject and there is not space here for it. We advise readers to follow up this general theme through their various boards. We introduce the discussion that we may urge generous support for all accredited Christian agencies centering in San Fran-

Wonderful Outlook

cisco. That city is to become one of the greatest of all time. Providence and its providential harbor determine that. In English-speaking work the Church meets difficulties there faced in no other city of America. Protestantism in San Francisco is pivotal and world-embracing. Let the Church comprehend that fact and she will make it her spiritual Gibraltar facing the East.

Forces in Array

Buddhism on the Pacific Coast

Japanese Buddhist missions expend forty thousand dollars per year to plant that faith on the Pacific coast. This is probably twice what any Protestant Church appropriates for Japanese work there. Buddhism has a finer headquarters building in Fresno, California, than any mission building of the most numerous Protestant body operating on the coast. It has cultured men. Next door to a Protestant mission in San Francisco is a Buddhist mission. This, by way of illustration, shows that great as is otherwise our task there, yet it is intensified, because the heathen world is not quiescent. The Orient invades our western coast with its religions and is aggressive.

Stupendous World Openings

The Church of God does right nobly, but did any body of people in any age live in such a

The West Between and Beyond

world at home, and face such a world Pacificward as do we just now? The situation is as glorious as stupendous. Nothing but our best will save other races and ourselves. We rise or fall together. We cannot leave this for another generation. It will be determined before then. The battle is on. America is the fortress. Who wins America wins ultimate world-capitulation.

QUESTIONS ON CHAPTER IV

AIM: TO REALIZE THE URGENT CALL TO THE CHURCH FROM THESE RAPIDLY GROWING STATES

1.* Name some of the advantages that San Francisco as a harbor has at present over Puget Sound.
2. Name the states included in the discussion of this chapter.
3. Compare the area of Colorado with that of England and Scotland.
4. Compare the area of Utah with Ohio and Tennessee.
5. Compare the area of Wyoming with Oregon.
6. Which one of these states in this section most resembles in its products Pennsylvania?
7.* Do you believe that it will be able to support a population as dense as Pennsylvania? Why?
8. In which state of these two sections, the Northwest and the West, would you prefer to live, and why?

9.* Which one of these two sections has the greater commercial resources and possibilities? Give reasons.
10.* Do you believe these western states can sustain as large a population per square mile as the states east of the Mississippi River? Give reasons.
11. What will be the population of the United States when the section west of the Mississippi River is as densely populated as the section east of the Mississippi River?
12. Name the factors that are the most influential in increasing the population.
13.* Which is the more permanent, an agricultural or a mining community? Why?
14. Where in the Bible do the Mormons find a basis for their religion?
15. Why would you prefer not to have your sister brought up in a polygamous household?
16. Why is Mormonism un-American?
17. On what grounds is Mr. Smoot allowed to hold his seat in the United States Senate?
18. Contrast this sect in its social and religious spirit and teaching with Christianity.
19. Why do you suppose this sect has made such progress in the United States?
20. What lessons can Christians learn from the Mormons?
21. Why has the Church of Christ not done more to Christianize the Mormons?
22. After reading this chapter in which section do you think missionary work is most needed?

23. What type of Christian effort is most in demand?
24.* Why cannot a wealthy state like Colorado finance its own home mission work?
25.* Give as many reasons as you can for immediately occupying these sections for Christ.

REFERENCES FOR FURTHER STUDY
CHAPTER IV[1]

I. *Colorado.*
Clark: Leavening the Nation, XI.
Drake: The Making of the Great West, 308-314.
Mills: "Economic Struggle in Colorado." Arena, February, '06; March, '06; May, '06; October, '06.
Smythe: The Conquest of Arid America, Part III, Chapter II.

II. *Wyoming.*
Clark: Leavening the Nation, X.
Smythe: The Conquest of Arid America, Part III, Chapter VIII.

III. *Mormons and Mormonism.*
Clark: Leavening the Nation. XV.
Davis: "Practical Results of Mormonism." Missionary Review of the World, March, '07.
Drake: The Making of the Great West, 264-268.
Guernsey: Under Our Flag, 132-160.
Horwill: "Investigation of the Mormon Church." Albany Review, June, '07.
Kinney: "Present Situation Among the Mormons." Missionary Review of the World, August, '06.
Smythe: The Conquest of Arid America, Part II, Chapter I.

---
[1] Current magazines should be consulted for other references on these subjects.

THE NEW SOUTHWEST

The Southwest is different from all other parts of the country. The Anglo-Saxon is everywhere else in the ascendant. Here the Latin races are dominant. It is astonishing to find so many oldest churches all over the country. The superlative is a national trait. We have either the oldest or the youngest, the greatest or the smallest, or the only thing in the world. However, it is almost certain that the oldest church and house are to be found in Santa Fé. The Church of San Miguel was built seventy years before the landing of the Pilgrims, and the house next to the church fifty years. It is the oldest settled, is the furthest behind, has the most Church-members per capita, and is the most ignorant and superstitious part of the land. In one part Mormonism holds sway. In the other Roman Catholicism of two centuries ago is still the prevailing religion.

—Puddefoot

Place the 50,000,000 inhabitants of the United States in 1880 all in Texas, and the population would not be as dense as that of Germany. Place them in New Mexico, and the density of population would not be as great as that of Belgium. Those 50,000,000 might all have been comfortably sustained in Texas. After allowing, say 50,000 square miles for "desert," Texas could have produced all our food crops in 1879—grown, as we have seen, on 164,215 square miles of land—could have raised the world's supply of cotton, 12,000,000 bales, at one bale to the acre, on 19,000 square miles, and then have had remaining, for a cattle-range, a territory larger than the state of New York. Place the population of the United States in 1890 all in Texas, and it would not be as dense as that of Italy; and if it were as crowded as England this one state would contain 129,000,000 souls.

—Strong

V
THE NEW SOUTHWEST

It is so new that one hardly knows where to begin the story. It is as lusty as new. The decided advance has been since 1900 and the remarkable acceleration is within three years. The Southwest includes Arizona, New Mexico, Oklahoma, and Texas. Arkansas and western Louisiana have characteristics similar to these four commonwealths. *[Decided Advance]*

Natural Domain and People in the Large

These six divisions have as much territory as France, Germany, and Austria-Hungary, which have a population of 150,000,000. The Southwest has 7,000,000. It is predicted that men now living may see 75,000,000 there. It is called the land of sunshine and opportunity. In one year New York recorded 118 cloudy days and El Paso, Texas, 36. *[Extent and Possible Population]*

When Arizona and New Mexico are admitted as states they will rank in size in the order named, four and five, and Nevada will *[Size of Arizona and New Mexico]* be moved from four down to six. It is as far across Arizona and New Mexico from east to west as from New York to Chicago.

Oklahoma and Texas

Oklahoma more than equals in area New England and Delaware, leaving out Maine, while Texas, which extends southward almost as far as does Florida, could be sliced into four and two-third Iowas.

Present Growth of the Southwest

The most rapid development in the Union is just now going on in the Southwest.[1] The home missionary situation is nowhere more acute and more freighted with destiny. In the decade ending with 1900 the center of population advanced but ten miles westward, but the growth of the Southwest drew it three miles southward. One hundred thousand a month is its increase in population. Home-seekers' excursions are frequent. Trains are so filled as to necessitate several sections. The people are ninety-six per cent. American. They come from between the Appalachians and the Mississippi.

Accessions from Cities

Texas and Oklahoma are now receiving larger accessions than any other states. Those who come to the Southwest are, generally speaking, experts in the selection of land and in

---

[1] Harvey, *Metropolitan Magazine*, August, 1908.

its tillage. Many are from the cities. A perceptible current from the city toward the soil is significant.

In Roosevelt County, New Mexico, where in 1900 no one lived, there are now homes on two thousand quarter sections. The Imperial Valley, Arizona, has doubled its people within one year and now has twenty-five thousand.

Samples of Increase

Nature in the Southwest, as elsewhere west of the Mississippi, has worn a forbidding aspect. This has turned men to other parts of the country. When, however, the divine purpose ripened, the government, the agricultural college, and railway development all conspired to unlock and advertise dormant treasures so long disguised.

Treasures Disclosed

Religious Foundations

If American Protestantism were to center in the Southwest all its home missionary energies at present employed in different parts of the United States, it would find there an ample field. Denominational destinies are being swiftly determined. A locality is quick to appreciate the Church which begins its ministry among the people when most it is needed, that is, at the beginning.

Pioneer Mission Service

Investing in Foundations

A denomination which stays with the people in their days of adversity is the Church of their choice in the years following. In proportion as a mission board provides for rural communities is its later work in the cities prosperous. City churches are largely built up out of small towns. A general officer of a prominent body complains that in a wide section of the West his Church is almost without a following. He gives as a reason their pioneer neglect of rural communities there. The type of Protestantism to which the Southwest will respond and which will become the Church of its adoption is the type that not only selects advantageous centers where conditions are least primitive, but which also starts with the people at the bottom and builds itself into their daily stress and struggle. Whatever Church is to figure largely in the Southwest must begin now. It must invest largely and contribute its highest type of men. It will reap what it sows. A hesitating administration will prove disastrous.

Results from Earlier Sowing

In all the years of initial missionary growth in the Southwest, years in which a rough frontier life seemed but little responsive to the labors of consecrated men, these faithful souls rested in the assurance that God's Word would not return void. Now, like a field well ploughed and carefully sown, the Southwest everywhere is responsive to former spiritual tillage. The old-timers remark upon the transformation.

The saloon is becoming unpopular. It is not so long ago that bull-fights in Arizona contributed to the building of a cathedral. Now gambling has been swept clean from both Arizona and New Mexico, while Texas comes forward with its new antigambling laws. The sentiment for intellectual improvement is positive and school privileges are excellent. The rough element in life retires. It is no longer in good form. *[Reform Tendencies]*

While these signs of encouragement, born of early missionary labors, are seen in the older settled communities, yet almost everything is to be done in the rapidly forming newer settlements. Reenforcements all out of proportion to those in the older towns are imperative. While most of the people may have lived elsewhere in a Christian community, yet their removal to a region where all is new tends to unsettle the foundations of spiritual life. They are completely absorbed in the preliminary struggle of existence and in establishing homes *[Interests of the Newer Settlements]* and surroundings which must be built in virgin newness from the ground up.

Prompt Action Will Prevent Drifting

The community is without precedents. Without strong anchorage it will drift. Without a positive dominating spiritual leadership it will not progress morally. We inherit so much in standards and observances which have become parts of a fixed order, that we are unconscious of these shaping influences of life and character. In a new settlement there is little moral background or perspective, hence the necessity for the most effective agencies. Mediocre men and measures may prove harmful as they prejudice the situation against future well-directed efforts. This is all to show that what is done for the Southwest should be done now, and that efforts lacking in statesmanship and resources will prove a disappointment. Spiritual experiments will not fit a situation marked by tremendous material certainties.

Mexicans and Indians

In sections where Mexicans and Indians are numerous, advance is retarded. The Indians, for the most part inoffensive and industrious, present needs calling for efforts as purely missionary as in the foreign field. This is also true of the Mexicans who are much of a dead lift.

Missions thoroughly manned among these peoples are fruitful, but they present conditions in sharp contrast to the work among Americans.

Arizona

Arizona is spoken of as a land apart. Its air suggests the great Sahara Desert or that of Mount Sinai, Arabia. The territory is divided by cliffs running diagonally northwestward. The northern part has an elevation of about six thousand feet, with pine forests covering ten thousand square miles. Arizona has the largest untouched forest in the United States. The southern part of the territory offers great opportunities for settlement, as irrigation has wrought changes there more wonderful than in any other part of the United States. A climate almost tropical coöperates with a soil like that of the Nile Valley. *Features of Arizona*

Arizona is a little larger than Italy with its population of thirty-three millions of people and but little smaller than the United Kingdom of Great Britain with forty-three millions. The annual rainfall is less than seven inches, but it has ten millions of acres susceptible of irrigation. Arizona stands most in need of conserving its streams and, providentially, conditions *Population and Water-Supply* are most favorable to that end. The Roosevelt Reservoir will be one hundred feet higher than Niagara Falls.

Conditions To Be Met

Living expenses are very high. This necessitates missionary appropriations larger than for other sections of the country. This is equally true of several parts of the Southwest. A railway from Phœnix to Los Angeles opens new territory where towns are building. Immediate attention bestowed there will richly repay missionary investment.

A Typical Town

An Arizona town in the southern part may illustrate conditions. It has 17,500 people, half of whom are Mexicans and Indians. Classed with the Americans are many Jews and Roman Catholics. One third of the influential people are Jews. Not more than one fourth of the Americans are interested in Church matters. This means that the normal field of operations is among but one eighth of the population. In the building of a fine church, apart from some aid by local banks, not more than two hundred dollars was secured in the town outside the denomination itself. The illustration shows how, in the initial stages, missionary aid is necessary.

Stimulating City Opportunities

A preacher who may command a large hearing and occupy a place of influence in one of

The New Southwest 161

these cities will succeed almost anywhere in the United States. The intellectual atmosphere is stimulating, as the brightest and most progressive young business men from all parts of the country carry on the enterprises and fill the professions. There is much latitude in religious thinking and a spirit of toleration. Materialism, however, strongly dominates. A manly, vigorous thinker, well equipped and spiritually endowed, will find in such a ministerial field one after his own heart.

Concerning Health-Seekers

In passing, we refer to a matter incidental to our subject but important. Many people journey to the Southwest in search of health. It would seem that some are not informed before going concerning the climate. While there is much sunshine and the air has all the curative properties ascribed to it, yet in the winter months the extremes of temperature demand about the same comforts and protection one needs in the eastern states. Many who go there, with but the shelter of a tent, must certainly endure hardships. Increased cost of living makes ordinary home essentials the more difficult to obtain. One who goes there to re-

Cautions to Health-Seekers

gain health will find it desirable to be well provided with funds.

Christian Ministrations Frontier churches in some localities, in addition to their efforts to maintain religious work, not always self-supporting, find in their midst a parish of transient health-seekers whose discomforts may heavily tax the sympathy and ministrations of local societies. And, while the personnel may change, the number may not lessen. Pastors of missionary churches receive letters asking that special attention be given some loved one temporarily residing there. The churches and pastors seek to minister tenderly to the many sick always with them.

Need of Church Hospitals Reference is made to this, in its relation to home missions, that the Church generally may inform itself concerning this extensive need. Church hospitals for tuberculosis, properly located, will prove of untold service.

Problems Connected With the Sick Home missionary work in the Southwest has been retarded because many of the churches have been supplied with pastors who were there to recuperate. These men were servants of God and their heroic struggle to regain health was in every way commendable, but they were not able to push the work where most it needed reenforcement. This condition is now largely eliminated. It emphasizes the need already mentioned of sanitariums in localities where the Church may properly care for its members, hundreds of whom might be restored to health by such beneficent ministry.

New Mexico

New Mexico embraces features of our oldest American civilization. Santa Fé claims priority in age over other cities in the United States. An old church there, said to have been reared in 1540, has a bell bearing the date 1351. An adobe house near at hand is pointed out as older than the church. *(Early New Mexico)*

The old and the new blend in New Mexico, but the new takes on remarkable vigor. Twenty thousand homes occupying two millions of acres have been established in a part of that territory in a single year. In twelve months the number of post-offices advanced from three hundred and twenty-two to five hundred and twenty-three. The new life of New Mexico is emphatically modern. This is seen in the character of its rapidly building towns. *(Rapid Modern Growth)*

One misses nothing of the recent and the best in conveniences of living. Churches planted in growing centers cannot be less at- *(Quick Returns for Churches Planted)* tractive than those in similar towns elsewhere. Missionary appropriations that might have proved effective five years ago will now entirely fail to command the situation. The conditions to be overcome are similar to those mentioned as existing in Arizona. The aid, however, while it must be substantial, is needed but for a little time. An able preacher backed by a home mission board will soon have a prosperous self-supporting church, whose perennial contributions toward the work of the board which nurtured it will reimburse the treasury many times its initial investment.

The Pecos Valley

The Pecos Valley in the southeastern part presents a new development which, in complete transformation and extent, will satisfy any one who is at all interested in an ideal home mission field. In 1890 only lean cattle found subsistence there. Now its numberless artesian wells water a soil that can be cultivated almost continuously. Sugar-beets raised here show the highest per cent. of beet-sugar known. One apple orchard produced a seventy thousand dollar crop. This extensive valley within two years will be densely populated.

Population and Resources

New Mexico at the last census had two hundred thousand people. It has now probably

MAIN STREET OF AN OKLAHOMA TOWN, AUGUST SIXTH
MAIN STREET OF SAME TOWN AUGUST SIXTEENTH
MAIN STREET OF SAME TOWN NOVEMBER SIXTH, SAME YEAR

The New Southwest 165

twice that number and is expected to reach a half million by 1910. Among the natural resources of New Mexico are one and a half millions of acres of coal land and five millions of acres of timber. In the northwest is a wide section, now remote from railways, but with natural resources certain to bring a large population. Missionary workers will do well to keep this part of New Mexico well within their angle of vision.

Oklahoma

Oklahoma is so recent to history that those born the year it was admitted as a territory are still in their 'teens. It is not seventeen years from the lonely haunt of the jack rabbit and coyote to a land filled with magnificent farms, bustling towns, sooty mines, and smoking industrial plants. *Oklahoma's Development*

Oklahoma for the next few years presents one of the exceptional opportunities of Christendom to strongly entrench Christianity. The Church that does not at once become strongly aggressive there will find later beginnings difficult. The growth in population and railway extension is unparalleled for the same period. *The Church's Opportunity*

No other state has been admitted to the Union with so many inhabitants. It now has *Growth of Population and Towns* one million five hundred thousand and is able to support five millions more. It is difficult anywhere in the state to get farther than twenty-five miles from a railway. The opening up of the "Big Pasture" is one of the latest attractions. This means a whole section of country preempted by a thrifty American people. Churches should immediately dot that region. Cities and towns are substantial, although their growth is phenomenal. Oklahoma City, the distributing center, had in 1900 about ten thousand people. To-day it has forty thousand. Seven cities have populations of ten thousand or more. There are thirty-five towns of between twenty-five hundred and ten thousand. Three towns in the southwest part of the state have grown in four years from nothing to four thousand, six thousand, and eight thousand respectively. There are sixteen hundred and fifty-two towns on the map. Oklahoma has accomplished in fifteen years what it took Kansas forty years to attain.

A Strategic State

Oklahoma is strategic. Its climate and soil would alone make it influential, but its central location and accessibility ordain it a potential commonwealth from which will emanate lines of communication to many parts of the country. There is nowhere such an intermingling of northern and southern people. Its Church life will be cosmopolitan. Its Christianity will, of necessity, have large vision, which means the missionary spirit. The foreign field may find here another strong base of supply.

Wide Range of Products

Oklahoma's location gives it agricultural possibilities for products of both a temperate and semitropical climate. Three fourths of its land is adapted to cotton and four fifths of it to wheat. It may now rank as fourth among cotton states. A writer says that Oklahoma can supply the West with cotton goods made in its own mills run by natural gas. It can furnish illuminating oil to the Northwest, and pave the cities of the Union with its asphalt.

Progress Since 1900

Since 1900 Oklahoma's factories have doubled, the output has tripled, and the capital invested quadrupled. She has more banks than Kansas and Nebraska combined. She publishes five hundred and seventy-five newspapers and periodicals. Her one hundred and five thousand Indians, real and theoretical, are outnumbered by whites fourteen to one.

A Call for Energetic Action

It is estimated that three fourths of the men and boys and half of all the people are outside any religious body. There are many Indians, but the problem is that of whites, as the Indians will be largely absorbed. The mission boards are awake to the situation. They are endeavoring to arouse the Church to a sense of what is passing. An insistent call comes to one of the boards for aid in building twenty churches. Two hundred and fifty dollars each will insure their erection, as the larger part of the money will be contributed locally. To secure results initial donations are necessary, as settlers who build homes on new soil often find their resources overdrawn. A few strong men placed just now in southwestern Oklahoma, at a cost to the boards of about five hundred dollars each, to supplement self-support in the local church, will mean a great return to the denomination which has the foresight and liberality to make the investment. Conditions in Oklahoma are stable, with no likelihood of a backward movement.

Texas

Texas an Imperial State

To even outline Texas is an ambitious task. One can draw a straight line for nine hundred miles within the state. Along with Oklahoma it shows the present high-water mark of advancement in the United States. It ranks fifth in population. It is predicted that by 1950 its people may number thirty millions. Texas and Oklahoma are destined to become our empire states both in people and material output.

Years ago Texas gave eastern capitalists ten counties in the Panhandle to build its state capital. The capitalists erected a fine structure and now their reward is a large one. This land, held for grazing, with ten acres or more needed for each steer, is now found to be good wheat soil. Everywhere in Texas, as in the Panhandle, the great ranches are being surveyed into farms. The purchaser may secure what land he needs down to ten acres. The inrush of settlers is bewildering. Along one railroad for a distance of one hundred and fifty miles but five families lived a little time ago, now more than twenty thousand heads of families are there, four fifths of whom came in twenty months. *Present Inrush of Settlers*

Texas now produces sixty-three varieties of agricultural products. In the southeastern part along the Rio Grande, a hundred miles inland, a rare quality of sugar-cane is grown. It will heavily affect the world's sugar market. Thousands of acres in the vicinity of Corpus Christi are turned to prolific truck patches where, throughout the winter, the landscape is green *Great Variety of Products* with the finest garden produce for northern markets. The Bermuda onion yield is enormous. This land a short time since sold for a dollar and fifty cents an acre. The oil output of southwest Texas annually foots up millions of barrels.

El Paso

El Paso in the extreme southwest is on the borders of Texas, New Mexico, and Mexico. It is a port of entry from Mexico. While it is an old city its forty-three thousand population has mostly been gathered within a few years. It is the largest city for five hundred miles east, north, or west, and for fifteen hundred miles south. It is the commercial gateway to Arizona, New Mexico, and west Texas. As a home missionary center its importance is not likely to be overestimated. Several denominations have recently erected fine churches there.

Railways of Texas Centering at Galveston

For forty years, up to 1905, Illinois led in total railway trackage. Now Texas leads with twelve thousand five hundred miles and has nearly five times the area of Illinois in which to expand. Galveston is one of the most promising cities. With its proximity to the Panama Canal, with the teeming Southwest at its back, with a growing network of railways to transport to its harbor the countless resources of mines and acres, who will forecast the future of Galveston?

The Wide Outlook

As the Northwest culminates in Puget Sound, and the West Between in San Francisco, so the Southwest will find its gateway through Galveston to the Panama Canal. This means the Southwest pouring itself out upon the Orient and western South America. We now have less to do with South America than with Asia. The Panama Canal lessens the distance from New York to Asia by seven thousand miles, but Galveston, nearer even than New Orleans, has by location large advantages over New York in freight passing through the divided Isthmus. *[Gateway to the Panama Canal]*

The startling changes wrought by great currents of trade, soon to spring from the Southwest and to flow through the Panama Canal, are difficult to predict. That they will surpass all present anticipations of the Church is certain. Protestantism should, without loss of time, scan and study the Southwest and be ready for the tide that is rising in that country. *[The Church Should Prepare for the Tide]*

Why is Porto Rico a new sister to our Southwest? And why for so long a time have we *[Our Neglect of Latin America]* been on little more than speaking terms with our older sister, South America? Longingly she and Latin America have looked our way. They have fashioned some twenty-one republics since ours was born. They have had a hard time with their various violent internal disorders. We have been neighborly enough to afford protection by gesticulating toward would-be foreign intruders so that they have been made to understand; but, on the whole, we have been so busy with our growing family and setting them all up in housekeeping that we have left South America much to herself.

South American Advancement
South America, with more than twice the area of the United States and with its thirty-five millions of people, has in the last few years advanced with giant strides. Governments there are becoming stable. Many parts of their continent rival the most progressive of our own land. We can learn of Brazil and the Argentine Republic concerning public improvements. The productive power of the people rapidly increases and we are told that South America is a country of such vast and varied resources as to need the surplus capital of both America and Europe for its development.

Mark the location and tilt of South America.

The New Southwest

Boston is on a direct line with Valparaiso on the west coast. "The principal ports of the western coast of South America will be from 60 to 1,700 miles nearer to New York than to San Francisco." South America pushed straight north would about fit into our east coast. On the west coast note Chili with its singular history and its tremendous awakening, as if it were in a competitive race to be abreast of Texas at the Isthmian Canal opening.

What does all this mean? No man may now fully answer, but any one may direct his vision to outstanding headlines pointing unmistakably the way of our future. Glance again northwestward. About and contributory to Puget Sound is wheat, wheat. Why were not the millions on millions of acres, yellow with bread for Asia, located elsewhere than in a territory seemingly made to order, to fit a world harbor specially constructed to float commissary fleets to an eastern hemisphere?

The Northwestward Outlook

And in the Southwest is Galveston, backed again by wheat. Yes and more. Texas alone can supply the world with one fifth more cotton than now grows on the whole globe. Cotton, not wool, is what clothes the eastern world. Again, Texas and Louisiana feed man-

The Southwestward Open Door

kind with three quarters of all the rice eaten, and they stand ready to produce every kernel now grown, a full present-day ration of rice for India, China, Japan, and every other land.

Molded for a Mission

Look at the map, and note how little territory lopped off at the northwest would have cut out Puget Sound. Again, look at Texas. Why is it elongated and sharpened in the direction of the Panama Canal? One may answer that the Rio Grande was made the boundary line and determined this elongated Texas. True, but why was not the continent so molded that the river would have emptied into the Gulf farther north and left more rice and cotton country on the Mexican side of the line? Texas then would not appear on the map as if it had been gripped by a Hercules and stretched to a point extending far southward in an effort to make it meet something.

The Export Trade

You answer, this was to give Galveston a wide sweep of country that it might be a mighty export city, the second of the United States, outranked only by New York. And why do the lands radiating from that particular port nearest the Panama Canal, groan with their profusion of cotton, rice, and wheat? And why were not the lands located elsewhere?

The New Southwest 175

Why is a rice-raising expert, to whom rice-growers go for ideas, located with his model plantation in Texas? And is there any significance in his being an Oriental, a distinguished Japanese? A colony of Japanese devoted to rice culture are there. One of them owns 1,600 acres. He is also one of the wealthiest land-owners in Japan. He may vote in his own country, because of the class to which he belongs, for a representative to the House of Peers. He employs expert farmers from Japan as foremen. His white neighbors are his laborers. Another Japanese of our Southwest has been a member of the Japanese House of Representatives and also principal of the noted Japanese educational institution founded by Neesima. The Chinese are there, good farmers, getting the best from rich land. Why is it that Orientals, both in the Northwest and in the Southwest fringe our export harbors to Asia? *Japanese and Chinese Experts*

Again, why is the most phenomenal railway development of the Union in Texas, and all available for Galveston? Then mark the time element. Why was Texas awakened into this amazement of production at about the time the Panama Canal was started? Why did the rail- *A Superhuman Purpose* way fever in Texas break out at about the same time? Why did Galveston rise from its overwhelming disaster of a few years ago and build as if dominated by a superhuman purpose? Was there a conscious Panama Canal motive which actuated the human side of these well-timed movements? To affirm that such was the case might be ridiculous. But is it unreasonable to suggest that back of all this there may be a "purpose, which is purposed in the earth"?

A Jewish Factor

It may be permissible to note that in the Southwest Jews are numerous. In various cities they direct and dominate large business interests. Study the relation of the Jews to the growth of Galveston and its commerce. Mark their present influence in endeavoring to make it a harbor of entry for immigrants as well as a port of world trade. And then, as in your thought all radiating lines of commerce become luminous because of the Christ who maps them and makes them bearers of his proclamation to the nations, you may recognize that in this new dispensation Israel once more appears and that the rejected Messiah still gives to his countrymen a place of honor in his imperial advance.

"The touch of race on race across the Pacific grows warmer every day. Through the channels of trade, through the sending over of hundreds of young men into educational work in the Orient, through the contact opened up by their looking to us for professional instruction and through an ever-growing travel, the touch of life on life becomes more intimate. The only safety for the awakening people in the Philippines, in China, and in Japan is to fill these channels with the water of life, as well as with the secular freight they bear.

Touch of Race on Race

"Paul saw a man of Macedonia beckoning him to bring the gospel over into Europe. We cannot estimate the results to-day of his obedience to that heavenly vision. There stands over against . . . us . . . a man forty times as great as Paul's man, beckoning us to bring the gospel over into Asia. He calls to us: 'Make your whole coast an apostle to the Gentiles. Fill the heads of your people with Paul's gospel and their hearts with his love, and then, through the touch of your commercial, political, social, educational and religious life upon ours, come over into Asia and help us.' "[1]

A New Macedonian Call

---
[1] Dr. Charles L. Thompson.

The Frontier

QUESTIONS ON CHAPTER V

AIM: To Realize the Call to the Church in the Rapid Development of the Southwest

1. Name the states included in this section.
2. How do France, Germany, and Austria-Hungary compare with the Southwest in area?
3. How does Texas compare with Germany in area, population, and possible resources?
4. How does Arizona compare with Nevada in area, population, and possible resources?
5. How many times can Pennsylvania be superimposed on Texas?
6. How does Oklahoma compare with France in climate?
7. Name the chief products of the Southwest.
8.* Do you believe the Southwest has greater commercial possibilities than the Northwest? Give reasons.
9. To which state in the Southwest would you prefer to go as a farmer? Why?
10. To which state in the Southwest would you prefer to go as a business man? Why?
11. How do the Northwest and Southwest compare in area and population?
12. Name the states that offer a good climate for tuberculosis patients.
13. Can a state be expected to care for invalids from other states?
14. Are the newly-established churches able to provide for the care of invalids from other sections?

The New Southwest

15. By what agency are hospitals for consumptives to be established?
16.* Name the factors that are contributing most to the development of the Southwest.
17.* What is the dominating motive among men in entering these new sections?
18.* Why is the Church less aggressive than commercial enterprises?
19. What do you consider some of the greatest temptations in a new community?
20. Give some examples of high moral ideals in these states?
21.* Is an old established or a new community most easily influenced? Why?
22.* In which section of the West do you believe there is the greatest need for Christian workers now? Give reasons.
23. To which state would you prefer to go as a Christian worker? Why?
24.* Which section do you consider the most strategic in its relationship to foreign countries and why?
25.* Sum up as carefully as you can the immediate need for home missionary workers.

REFERENCES FOR FURTHER STUDY
CHAPTER V[1]

I. *The Southwest.*

Harvey: "The Great Southwest." Munsey's Magazine, March, '05.

---
[1] For additional references, see Bibliography, pages 265-279

Matson: "The Awakening of Nevada." Review of Reviews, July, '06.
Ogden: "Farming in the Southwest." Everybody's Magazine, November, '07.
Puddefoot: The Minute Man on the Frontier, XXII.
"The Growth of Southwest Texas." Review of Reviews, February, '06.

II. *Texas.*

Bessey: "Vegetation of Texas." Science, April 19, '07.
Cunniff: "Texas and the Texans." World's Work, March, '06.
Mowry: The Territorial Growth of the United States, V.

III. *Oklahoma.*

Clark: Leavening the Nation, XI.
Cunniff: "The New State of Oklahoma." World's Work, June, '06.
Hough: "Rise of the State of Oklahoma." Appleton's Magazine, April, '07.
McGuire: "Big Oklahoma." National Geographic Magazine, February, '06.

THE AMERICAN INDIANS AND SOME OTHER PEOPLES

Much that was vicious in the administration of Indian affairs has been eliminated during recent years. The system of Indian education was never better, never more liberally supported by the government, and in allotting good land in severalty to Indians whose reservations still contain good land, we are fulfilling our obligation to those individual Indians. But from the portion of the nation's trust which fell into the political pot we have the barren reservations, perpetuated for many thousands of Indians of the second and third generation whom we must, perforce, continue to support, or "civilize" as railroad section hands and ditch diggers and sellers of bead-work, while the white man cultivates their good land. We now show a belated eagerness to square ourselves with these Indians by allotting to them their choice of land from the poor remnants which have been left to them after the many choosings of the white man—a pathetic spectacle, this granting Indians the choice of land on which no well-equipped white man could make a living. This portion of our great obligation is beyond redemption.

—*Humphrey*

However future legislation may affect the numbers of Chinese coming to America is no part of this discussion. Present facts and conditions are sufficient stimulus to greatest endeavor. The existence of so many Chinese now among us; the increasing number of native-born, who are eligible for citizenship; the great possibilities of the Chinese as individuals and as a people; the expediency and eternal rightness of cultivating friendly relations with neighboring nations; the unique position of America as the embodiment and exponent of the highest civil and religious life and institutions yet developed; the certainty that if we do not Christianize the Chinese they will paganize us—all these and other considerations impose obligations, responsibilities, and necessities which we cannot escape, and give us unequaled prestige and opportunity for evangelizing the Chinese.

—*James*

VI

THE AMERICAN INDIANS AND SOME OTHER PEOPLES

An obstruction in a stream indicates the swiftness of its current. Waters will flow. The obstruction opposes and there is commotion. The Indian has been stationary. Progress swept around and by him. The Indian objected. The stream foamed in agitation about him or swept him away. *Current and Obstruction*

Man and nature are coördinate. They rise or relapse together. The difference in nations is in their different relations to nature. Man cannot rise save by conquest of nature, and nature is raw and crude and wild until domesticated by man. Nature is the complement of man and reflects man. A pictured group of men will tell you their natural environment and a pictured landscape will indicate the kind of people living there. Paul tells how the perfecting of nature awaits the perfect man. "For the earnest expectation of the creation waiteth for the revealing of the sons of God. For we know that the whole creation groaneth and travaileth *Man Bound Up With Nature* in pain with us until now." Paul's full vision of the situation is set forth in verses eighteen to twenty-five of the eighth chapter of Romans.

Working Together

Man who acknowledges the kinship of nature, and devoutly yokes himself to her, and works in companionship with her and God, transforms both himself and nature. The wilderness is changed to an Eden, and the man is transfigured into a son of God.

Working Apart

Man may repudiate his higher relationship to nature and she will repudiate him. He remains a slave, for freedom comes only by conquest. She tells him no deep secrets. He lurks afraid, superstitious. His God even must be appeased. He is a barbarian, and lives in a wilderness. If you would see how far we have come, study a blanket Indian.

God the Key to Enlightenment

But nations know nature only as they know God. The gospel reveals God. Thus Christian nations are enlightened, free, powerful.

The Anglo-Saxon and America

When the early Anglo-Saxon came to this continent he at once proceeded to subdue it. He has been busy at it ever since. That struggle has made him the modern Anglo-Saxon, and he has made the United States of America. Neither could have been produced without the other. But this early Anglo-Saxon brought

God, the Holy Scriptures, and conscience with him. Could either this country or the typical American have been possible without obedience to God and the ten commandments? This question helps to measure the missionary and what we owe him.

Antipodal Races

The white man, when he landed, found the Indian in surroundings that had environed him for centuries. All present potentialities were there. And yet this red man had left almost no mark on his world. Had some plague silently divested this North American continent of every inhabitant, few signs would have remained, save in the Southwest, to indicate that the land was once inhabited. The Indian gave no challenge to nature, and both sulked in savagery. These two types of man meeting on this continent explain their antagonisms. *[The Indian and White Man]*

The antipodes met. How could they mingle? Not that their relationships might not have been more humane, not that the more enlightened should not have been more considerate and tolerant concerning his dusky brother. All this might have been, and many a page of our history be marked with beneficence rather than blood—would God it were so!—yet, in the out- *[Grapple With Nature Makes the White Race Supreme]* come, the whites would be a supreme and the Indians a subject race. Why? The paleface grappled with nature, the red man did not. This fixed the rank of each.

Opposing Principles

While we cannot excuse unholy antagonisms nor deny the Indian any just right, we may better interpret history if we hold this key, namely, that these two representatives of the race stood for principles as opposed as light and darkness, life and death. They could never blend; one must go down before the other. Suppose the white race had been driven into the sea and the aborigines had held the soil until now, what kind of a country would this be and what different direction would have been given to the history of the world?

A Course of Evolution

We must not be interpreted as in anywise excusing the white man where he might have accorded better treatment to the Indian; but we do well to keep in mind that this country was an evolution, and that its Indian policy was likewise an evolution.

Demand for Living Room

What White Occupancy Involved

Broadly speaking, the early settlers asked only living room. But this meant forests felled, roads, farms, mills, towns, wide communica-

American Indians and Other Peoples

tion—in short, the destruction of the wilderness. This in turn meant ruined hunting-grounds and the obliteration of primitive Indian life. The white man could not avoid this. The Indian could not permit it and remain an uncivilized Indian. In either case it was a grim struggle for self-preservation. The Indian resisted encroachment, the other fought for subsistence.

The intention of the white man was, on the whole, benevolent. As the stronger, his thought was not to annihilate the weaker. The two races could not mix, for no two ideals of living could be more antagonistic. What was essential to one was abhorrent to the other; therefore they agreed to live apart. The white man made a treaty. It provided hunting-grounds and wide domain for the Indian where he might live unmolested. *A Benevolent Intention*

Factors in the Field

But the Anglo-Saxon little dreamed the largeness of his future. In course of time a normal advance overflowed the Indian frontier. Dissensions followed, antagonisms were kindled, wars broke out. It was impossible for these two races to see alike. They looked in *Expansion of the White Race— Indian Stolidity* opposite directions. The Indian was always moved on, and every move might have been thought the last. The government again and again violated treaties, but, in most cases, the government met issues as unpremeditated as to the Indian they seemed unjust. Progress had come that far. It could not pause unless it changed its nature. The Indian sat stolidly smoking in front of his wigwam, squarely in the road of human advance. The Indian did not care to advance, he insisted on being let alone. This meant that humanity must double on its track backward toward barbarism.

Border Warfare

We cannot now easily appreciate that ever-recurring dilemma—the American Indian. That the border line of two such civilizations was that of border wars and bitter hostilities is not surprising. Taking humanity for what it is and was, taking savagery for what it may be, our colonial Indian history is not after all difficult to explain.

Efforts of Missionaries

These early annals are brightened by illustrious examples of Christian brotherhood toward the original inhabitants. David Brainerd, Eliot, Edwards, and others, choicest spirits of a noble race, gave themselves without stint to the uplift of the red man. The response

American Indians and Other Peoples 189

was proportionate to the sacrifice, and gave early pledge of the power of the gospel to save aborigines as well as the civilized.

These efforts were among the highest expressions of a heroic Church. Had they continued, relationships would have been more friendly, but never do we find the Indian rising to a position of nature conquest. At best he follows weakly and hesitatingly in the white man's tracks, and, save in his own element, he is a secondary race. Wars follow, and the conditions of life for generations tend to strenuous crudeness. Life was elemental—so formative, shifting, and new that the higher graces of thought for others with missionary zeal were hardly to be looked for; yet, that they flourished so extensively is indicative of the masculine Christianity of those times. Since then we have been preoccupied by internal development and an expansion beyond all thought of early Americans. Landmarks, limitations, and frontiers of those days were fitted to another age and country than the United States of to-day.

Working of Elemental Forces

Tribal divisions have made work among untamed inhabitants of the country difficult. There was no written language. This resulted in such variations of speech as to make it im-

Obstacles of Tribe and Language

possible for one tribe to understand another. It has been estimated that they employed two hundred different languages.

Numbers and Distribution

Present Indian Population

The present number of Indians, exclusive of Alaska, is from 250,000 to 300,000. While estimates differ concerning the aborigines in the country at the time of its discovery and later, some prominent authorities of to-day think the number has never been greater than now. The Indian is not dying out; his birthrate increases.

Distribution of Indians

Concerning the present distribution of the Indians and our national policy regarding them, we quote from Dr. S. H. Doyle. They are divided into seven classes as follows:

"1. *The Six Nations of New York.* These number about 5,500, and are but little removed from the simpler life of the poor whites of the state.

"2. *The Five Civilized Tribes.* These are the Cherokees, Chickasaws, Choctaws, Creeks, and Seminoles. They live in Indian Territory, and number nearly 67,000. The gospel has been preached and schools maintained among these tribes for generations, so that few traces of their native Indian life are seen among them to-day.

"3. *The Eastern Cherokees of North Carolina.* These refused to go westward with the great body of their sixty tribes years ago, but remained among the mountain homes of their forefathers. Their population is about 35,000.

"4. *Indians on Reservations.* These reservations are under the control of the national government, are not taxed or taxable, and are to be found in almost every one of the western states. The population of the reservations is over 125,000.

"5. *The Pueblos of New Mexico.* The ancestors of the Pueblos were a remarkable and ancient people. They were neither warlike nor migratory, but dwelt in houses, built of bricks, after a style of architecture peculiarly their own. The Pueblos number nearly 10,000.

"6. *The Apaches.* They consist of about 400 prisoners of war, under the War Department.

"7. *Imprisoned Indians.* These are in national, state, or territorial prisons. Their number is about 200.

Historical Survey

Periods of Governmental Relation

"The relation of the United States government to the Indian has been divided into three periods: the *colonial,* the *national,* and the *modern,* the last beginning with the presidency of General Grant.

Colonial Period

"The *colonial* period was characterized by constant wars, bloodshed, and rapine. The trouble arose mainly from the fact that the two races and civilizations, differing vastly in character, had been brought together on our shores with the coming of the white man. Yet the fact cannot be disguised that the most bloody Indian wars and massacres of colonial days were inspired by the whites themselves. The English and the French struggled for a century for supremacy in America, and in these struggles both nations and even the American colonists did not scruple to use the Indians as allies when sorely pressed. 'French tomahawks and scalping-knives struck down and mutilated English women and children, in the exposed settlements of Massachusetts, Pennsylvania, and Virginia. French officers were in command at Deerfield, at Fort William Henry, and at Braddock's defeat. Nor does history record that they put forth any effort to prevent the horrors perpetrated by the Indians. Nor was England in her hour of need more scrupulous.'

"The *national* period of the government's relation to the Indian has been called 'a century of dishonor.' Peace with the Indians was impossible, because of the insatiate greed of the settler for the Indian's land. To prevent settlement upon the lands allotted to the Indians was impossible. Washington tried it but failed. He recommended to Congress that 'no settlement should be made west of the clearly marked boundary line, and that no purchase of land from the Indians except by the government should be permitted.' This recommendation, however, was disregarded, and another Indian war was the result. In the earliest treaties made by the government with the Indians, where boundary lines were distinctly marked, the lands designated were given to the Indians *forever,* and white settlers were left to the mercy of the Indians for punishment. On January 21, 1785, such a treaty was made with the Ottawas, Chippewas, and Delawares. But these treaties were utterly disregarded by the whites, and the wars followed which resulted in the defeat of General St. Clair and the mas-

National Period

sacre of his troops, and in the victory of General Anthony Wayne over the Miamis. These wars are illustrative of every war that has occurred with the Indians from that time to this. Treaties were made, promising lands to the Indians, 'while water ran and grass grew.' The ink in which the treaty was written was scarcely dry before our unrestrained and unrestrainable settlers would proceed to violate their terms. This invariably led to irritation, and to individual acts of revenge on the part of the Indians, and then followed war.

Modern Period

"The *modern* period of our relations with the Indians began with the first term of General Grant as President. In 1870 he introduced what has been called 'The Peace Policy.' He announced his intention of dealing with the Indian question in a more just and friendly manner. He advocated their civilization, the education of their children, and the fulfilment of treaty obligations. He appealed to Christian bodies to assist in their amelioration. As a result of his policy the 'Indian Rights Association' was formed. It consists of nine members, for whose services no salary is paid. The work of the association is to 'spread correct information, to create intelligent interest, to set in mo-

American Indians and Other Peoples 195

tion public and private forces which will bring about legislation, and by public meetings and private labors to prevent wrongs against the Indian and to further good works of many kinds for him.' The 'Woman's National Indian Association' is a supplementary body, which deals philanthropically with the Indian as an individual. It establishes missions where there are none and turns them over to Christian denominations, who will care for them.

"The Peace Policy has produced splendid results. Indian outbreaks are less frequent. Military outposts have been abandoned, and some have even been turned into schools. Savage and barbarous customs are giving way to the forms of civilization. **Peace Policy**

"The Department of the Interior at Washington has charge of the government of the Indians. The Commissioner of Indian Affairs is at the head of the Indian office, which is a bureau in this department. About one half of the Indians to-day are on reservations—a term applied to the land set apart or reserved by the government for the exclusive use of the Indians. On each reservation is a government agent, who has associated with him a physician, clerk, farmers, policemen, and other employees, **Present Organization** all of whom are paid by the government. The entire establishment is called an Indian agency. The agents are responsible to the Commissioner of Indians, who is appointed by the President and resides in Washington.

Evils of Reservation System

"One of the worst features of the Reservation System is the distribution of rations. The reservations are not fitted for agriculture. The inhabitants have therefore to be fed by the government, which deals out rations periodically to many of the tribes. This is a vicious system. It breeds laziness and incapacity. It gives the Indian agent, if he be unscrupulous, a dangerous advantage over those for whom he should care, for he can give or withhold the rations, and thus has the very lives of the 'nation's wards' in his hands. The Indian by such a system never can be taught to become a self-respecting and self-supporting citizen.

Indian Education

"The education of the Indian boys and girls is receiving special attention by the government. It aims to educate them both industrially and intellectually. For this purpose it has established non-reservation boarding-schools, reservation boarding-schools, and reservation and independent day-schools. The Indians also attend state and territorial public

American Indians and Other Peoples

schools, contract day and boarding-schools, and mission day and boarding-schools. The object of Indian education is not so much to give a 'higher education' as it is to fit the boys and girls for the duties of every-day life. The course of instruction is patterned after that in our common schools, and to this is added industrial training. In the large non-reservation schools shoemaking, harness-making, tailoring, blacksmithing, plastering, and brickmaking and laying are taught with considerable effectiveness."

Recent Radical Change

Indian Citizenship

We have inserted this quotation at length as it concisely sums up the past and outlines the present policy down to the last three or four years. In that time radical changes have been introduced. They provide that the Indian as rapidly as possible shall pass from government tutelage and be placed like every other citizen face to face with nature and there fix his own status. The reason for this is fairly summed up in the following, quoted from Julia H. Johnston's *Indian and Spanish Neighbors:*

The "Last Man"

"When the best thing has been said for the Indian, he is to-day the last man. The immigrants landing at Ellis Island in three months outnumber the entire Indian population, and four times as many Porto Ricans as there are Indians have come under our stars and stripes. The negro question is forty times as great as the Indian question. But shall the red man be forgotten? Not if the Church has a message from God, for God forgets no man in his message."

Allotments and Industry

The Indian is to be absorbed within twenty-five years. He will be known only as an American citizen. The Dawes act of 1887, modified by the Burke law, provides that the Indians are to receive allotments of land, 160 acres each, and as soon as any show ability to manage their own affairs they are to receive title to the land and are clothed with the right to vote. More than half the Indians in the United States are now voters and have received their land allotments. Government education for the Indian began by an appropriation of $20,000 in 1877. The yearly amount is now nearly $4,000,000. Most judicious and painstaking efforts are made to secure work for the Indians on the railways, irrigation dams, in the sugar-beet fields, and elsewhere. They prove valuable helpers, and on the whole the labor demand is greater than the supply.

American Indians and Other Peoples 199

Protection from Intoxicants

An appropriation of $25,000 was made to protect the Indians of the Indian Territory against the illegal traffic in intoxicants. The work done by the government's agent and his helpers is most gratifying.

A Quarter Century of Honor

For the last twenty-five years our government has applied itself to the improvement of the red man as probably no other nation has ever devoted itself to the needs of a ward. Our Indian wrongs have been many and deep. To be understood they must be studied in their individual bearings; but concerning the present attitude and efforts of the government for the betterment of that race there can be no question.

Sympathy

This "last man" needs our sympathy because of the rapid and revolutionary changes that confront him. Their aim is beneficent but none the less confusing to the Indian.

Names and the Family Basis

The Indians are now being named so that a family record may be continuous. This means that the tribe disappears and the family becomes paramount. The most marked advance has been among the "Five Civilized Tribes" of Oklahoma—formerly a part of Indian Territory. A study of their progress and present status is important.

Indian Missions

Initial Barriers This brings us to the immediate and present bearing of missions on the Indian problem. A hindrance to missionary success has been the scandalous treatment of the aborigines by the whites. A sullen hatred met the white missionary. Considering the difficulties and the comparatively small number of Indians, missions among them have been successful beyond what might have been expected. A new era of Indian missions is now upon us.

Personal Standing Now the Aim We must meet our native brother in his new relationships. Family life, social obligations, business relationships, all are to have the same meaning to him as to any man. He is to be encouraged to stand alone and to learn that there is One only whom any man may safely trust for guidance.

Lifelong Workers Needed The demand is for recruits who will enlist for life, learn the language of the people to whom they go and there build a life-time of ministry into a new and changing order. The success of these missions in the past, with all the disadvantages of the reservation system or worse, is among the brightest annals of the kingdom.

BLANKET INDIAN EVANGELISTIC CONVENTION, CHISTEMAKO

At least eight Protestant denominations are engaged in this work. Our red neighbors are accessible. Possibly we cannot better summarize than to quote again from Julia H. Johnston:[1]

Eight Christian Bodies at Work

"An Indian chief wrote to a southern board of missions: 'God did not reject us. I hope his friends will not reject us. I hope your board will soon send a man in the name of Christ to come and seek and save the poor lost red man. We are distressed on every side. We want friends and help. Our last and only hope is in the Church of Christ. Our woes are heavy upon us.'

A Pathetic Plea

"Before the first missionaries came to Saddle Mountain, Oklahoma, the hearts of the Indians were steeled against all white men. Their objections to a government school were so great that another site was chosen. When the Great Father brought them a missionary, a little bit of a woman who could not defend her scalp against them for five minutes, they were mightily stirred, and said, 'We will let this Jesus woman sit down with us because the Great Father has sent her.'

Opposition Overcome

"At first they objected to 'the church road,'

"The Way Ahead Road"

[1] *Indian and Spanish Neighbors*, 83, 84.

and would have no building, fearing the 'bad white man' would come, but at last, some time after the organization of the missionary society, 'God's Light upon the Mountain,' they changed their minds about 'the church road' and called it 'the way ahead road,' which the teacher had showed them.

"Aim-day-co"

"Another lovely young teacher among these people was called by them 'Aim-day-co.' The Kiowa chief, Big Tree, thus explained the name: 'When we Kiowas see any one going the wrong road and into danger, we cry out, "Aim-day-co—Turn this way." Our sister saw us on the wrong road—she saw our great danger and called to us, "Turn this way. Turn to Jesus." Thus we call her "Aim-day-co." ' "

Inspiring Results

Bishop Ridley's Testimony

A comprehensive statement comes from the Episcopal Bishop of California, having supervision over an immense territory reaching to Alaska. Bishop Ridley says that he remembers "when there was not a Christian Indian from the tidal waters to the river sources among the mountains, but that now there is not a tribe without church, school, and a band of praying Christians.

"From that earlier to this later day, encouragements have continued. In December, 1904, the Indian population of South Dakota was 20,000. Of these 4,000 were communicants in about one hundred congregations of one denomination, some districts containing fifteen or twenty of these. In making a circuit of them the missionary is obliged to travel from two to four hundred miles. These Indian congregations gave last year $8,075.

South Dakota Communicants

"The Pima Church, in Sacaton, has a membership of 525 persons, the largest of any church in Arizona. This is one of seven gathered by that heroic missionary, Rev. Charles Cook, whose heart was so stirred by hearing of the Pimas from an army officer that in 1870 he gave up the pastorate of a German church under his care in Chicago and started out without pledge of support from any board and without money enough to pay his traveling expenses. He took a Bible, a rifle, a small melodeon, and some cooking utensils with him. While learning the language, he supported himself as a trader. For ten years his labors seemed vain, but now the results show 1,100 Christian Indians, and Mr. Cook requires nine helpers in his work, six of whom are Indians.

Cook in Arizona

In one house of worship the adults crowd the room at one service, and in the evening the children fill it. Only in this way, turn about, can the house accommodate the numbers. An onlooker reports, 'It may well be doubted if such a devout and worshipful audience can be duplicated in our land.'

A Wonderful Religious Gathering

" 'If there is anywhere in the United States at any time of the year a religious gathering which surpasses, or even equals, in interest the annual convocation of the Indian congregations of South Dakota I should like to know it,' writes one competent to speak.

" By This Sign Conquer"

"At this time about 2,000 people gather. There are ten departments, represented by delegates, and each company bears aloft a white standard with a cross, and the motto, 'By this sign conquer,' embroidered in different colors for each division. These great companies start from their several camps, fall into line before bishop and clergy and march to the place of meeting. A photograph of this great kneeling congregation, engaged in solemn worship on the vast level of the blue-arched prairie, red men and white together, brothers all, is a picture which once seen, though but in the compass of a leaflet, can never be forgotten.

American Indians and Other Peoples 205

Women's Offerings

"The representatives of ninety congregations gather to consider woman's work at this time, each delegate anxious to tell her story and to present the offering from her district. These gifts, at the last convocation, varied from three to five hundred dollars, and at the close of this memorable day those sisters in red had offered nearly $2,500 for the missionary work in South Dakota and elsewhere, at a sacrifice that meant many times what that amount would have cost white people in moderate circumstances. Less than thirty-five years of missionary work in this field by Bishop Hare and his clergy, with their wives, have changed the fierce, warlike heathen Sioux into these devout Christians.

Roosevelt's Address

"President (then Governor) Roosevelt's address at the Ecumenical Missionary Conference,[1] rehearsing his personal experiences among the Indians, stirs the pulse-beats even now, from the printed page:

Tribute to the Missionaries

"'I spent twice the time I intended to, because I became so interested . . . to see what was being done. It needed no time at all to see that the great factors in the uplifting of the Indians were the men who were teaching the Indian to be a Christian citizen. . . . No

[1] New York City, 1900. Report, Vol. I, 40-43.

more practical work, no work more productive of fruit for civilization, could exist than the work being carried on by men and women who give their lives to preaching the gospel of Christ to mankind.

Transformed Indians

" 'Out there on the Indian reservations you see every grade of the struggle of the last 2,000 years repeated, from the painted heathen savage, looking out with unconquerable eyes from the reservation on which he is penned, ... to the Christian worker of a dusky skin, but as devoted to the work, as emphatically doing his duty as given him or her to see it as any one here to-night. I saw a missionary gathering out on one of those reservations, ... not the same in grade but the same in kind, as that which is here to-night, and it was a gathering where ninety-nine per cent. of the people were Indians; where the father and mother had come in a wagon with the ponies, with the lodge-poles trailing behind them, over the prairie for a couple of hundred miles to attend this missionary conference. They were helped by the white missionaries, but they did it almost all themselves, subscribing out of their little all they could, that the work might go on among their brethren who yet were blind.

It was a touching sight to look at and a sight to learn from.

"'You who go out throughout the world realize that the best work can be done by those who do not limit the good work to their own immediate neighborhood, that the nation that spends most effort in trying to see that the work is well done at home is the one that can spare most effort in trying to see that duty is done abroad.' *The Altruistic Spirit*

"And yet—there are forty-two of the one hundred and sixty-five existent tribes who have not even heard of Christ." *Work Remaining*

Our Mexican Wards

Looking toward the Southwest we see 100,000 Mexicans; our inheritance with the soil annexed from Mexico. If one would see the contrast between the two civilizations, Mexican and American, let him step across from El Paso, Texas, into the Mexican town of Juarez on the opposite bank of the Rio Grande in Mexico. The two places might seem, save for certain modern marks, a thousand miles apart. Unrestricted gambling, squalor, and poverty is in open evidence. The Mexican lets to-morrow care for the things of to-day. Like *Another Undeveloped Race* the Indian, he must get his diploma from nature and earn it by the sweat of his brow. We must allow for heredity. The grade up which we have come is long and gradual. Generations are its milestones. We will not expect too much at once either of Mexicans or Indians. But the Mexican, where the investment in him is adequate, responds. Some sixty mission schools with one hundred and forty teachers are in New Mexico.

Encouraging Returns Thousands of Mexican people are Christians and scores of them are preaching the gospel. The schools, where boys and girls are adjusted to higher standards, are fundamental to future homes. Although state or government schools may be of a high order, yet the mission school fills an important place, as an essential to the curriculum of life is to know Christ and to be trained in the ways of modern living. These winsome, responsive children and these young people, how they appeal to the hearts of their teachers! As in other missions, we find work among the Mexicans owes most to a few lives who, for a generation or more, have given themselves to this people and now as a result they number faithful Christians by hundreds. This is exemplified in the forty years' service

ANGLO-JAPANESE TRAINING SCHOOL, SAN FRANCISCO, CALIFORNIA

JAPANESE BUDDHIST MISSION AND PASTOR, SAN FRANCISCO, CALIFORNIA

American Indians and Other Peoples 209

rendered by Dr. Thomas Harwood of Albuquerque, New Mexico. Well-equipped mission schools and a thoroughly organized mission territory, all under strong Anglo-Saxon leadership, are essential.

The Japanese

Japanese Openness to Progress — The Japanese are easily the best class of immigrants among recent arrivals. They represent the highest intelligence, the broadest outlook, and the most successful initiative of Asiatics coming to us. The upheaval in their own land and the liberating influences of Christianity and western civilization divorce the Japanese from dead tradition and leave them hospitable to all that humanity has to offer.

Passion for Learning — He is a born student. His passion for learning is phenomenal. His mental poise is equaled only by his dispassionate, analytical view of his surroundings. The Japanese percentage of illiteracy is the smallest among the newer immigration. His ideals are American, and he assimilates our civilization and modes of living as if born to them. He either cuts loose from his mother country or entertains the ambition to carry back to it what will help place it at the front among enlightened nations.

The Frontier

Industry and Business Acumen

His industry is monumental. He wins at a price few pay and is not conscious of sacrifice. His business ability is of the first order, and whether in the field of capital or labor he plans to fit in so as to produce least friction in our American life. His intelligence concerning the whole situation here is almost startling, and withal, if forced to defend his presence in this country, his statements are so sane, lucid, and modest as to make successful reply impossible. His manner of defense is equal to its matter.

Mostly in Hawaii

The Japanese began coming in 1866, with a total of seven persons. Most of them have arrived since 1900. The majority are in Hawaii. At least one tenth as many return each year as arrive. Their immigration to us is but one twenty-fifth of that of the Italians.

Very Small Increase

Japanese increase in immigration is insignificant as compared with other peoples. In five years, from 1902 to 1906, the total number of Japanese coming to the United States, and their distribution, is as follows: Hawaii, 44,503; California, 15,122; Oregon, 1,454; Washington, 9,504; other States, 3,559.

High Range of Pursuits

European immigration to the Pacific coast exceeds many times the Japanese. In 1906 there came but three Japanese to 191 Europeans.

American Indians and Other Peoples 211

About 63 out of each hundred Japanese are farmers and farm laborers; but their percentage of professional men is exceeded only by Germany. One in every eight is a skilled laborer. They show a larger number of merchants than those from any European country. Less than six per cent. of the Japanese are of that class of laborers who usually go to our cities. The amount of money they bring per capita is exceeded only by the Germans and English.

In 1906 but 84 Japanese were excluded as possibly liable to become a public charge. In the same year but one Japanese was received in our hospitals, while the lowest of any other foreign nationality was the Scandinavians, 179. Nearly 98 per cent. of Japanese immigrants are between the ages of 14 and 44. European immigration is from one tenth to one third infant and aged.

A Self-Supporting People

The Japanese laborers do not lessen the wages of their class. They are desirable from a mercantile standpoint. They buy 89 per cent. of their supplies in this country. They are peace-loving. Fifty per cent. of the inhabitants of the Hawaiian group are Japanese, and not the slightest trouble has arisen. They adopt

Adaptation to Our Social Structure

American methods of dress and living. They do not, as a rule, colonize in cities, but endeavor to establish independent homes for the purpose of bringing themselves quickly in touch with the native population.

Nobly Meeting the Earthquake Test

In San Francisco they were the first in the time of earthquake and fire to organize and cease to become recipients of public aid. Their plan of self-relief was more effective than any other. The Japanese government sent $25,000 to care for its own people. But $10,000 was used by them and the $15,000 is now held for a benevolent object. The Japanese Emperor also sent $100,000 for the general relief fund, very little of which went to the Japanese.

The Chinese

Problem of Chinese Evangelization

The evangelization of the Chinese people, whether in China or America, is a problem too great to be treated exhaustively in this chapter. A few salient points only can be set forth.

Their Distribution

Waiving all political and economic discussion, our work is with and for the Chinese as we find them in America. There may be in all about 70,000 Chinese here between the Atlantic and the Pacific. Fully half are on the Pacific Coast. In some large cities of the East

American Indians and Other Peoples 213

there are considerable colonies, and many smaller cities have also small squads.

The Chinese are a proud, conservative, self-satisfied people, with three religious systems of their own, and a highly organized civilization that has lived down all contemporaries for thousand of years; but, added to these inherent and initial difficulties to their accepting a new and exclusive faith, the Chinese are met, pursued, and surrounded with difficulties, restrictions, and indignities not shown to any other people. These are contrary to the spirit of our faith, and such as seriously to prejudice them against a faith that permits such practises upon a defenseless people. The mountain of difficulties they bring with them is climaxed by the artificial ones we heap upon them. *Race Characteristics and Ill Treatment*

Conditions of Christian work among the Chinese in America cannot be understood without some realizing sense of this handicap. Some people seem to think it useless to try. But Chinese are sensible, reasonable, religious, and practical, and they have learned two things: First, that the unchristian treatment they receive represents the passing sentiment only of the thoughtless and hoodlum elements, and is not the sober thought of the intelligent *Their Reasonable View* people of America, nor even of the Pacific Coast; second, that the Lord Jesus Christ "hath power on earth to forgive sins."

Christian Brotherhood

Chinese work among Chinese, in China and in America, is doing more than all other agencies combined toward harmonizing these two great peoples, by bringing multitudes of Chinese into spiritual fellowship and fraternity with ourselves, and by demonstrating to ourselves and to the world now that great truth which Peter and all the Apostles had to learn, that "unto the Gentiles (Chinese) also hath God granted repentance unto life."

Their Presence Not an Evil

The Chinese are not here as contract laborers and they are not servile. They come as free men. They do not depress wages, and in skilled labor they do not compete. They benefit white labor. They are not an inferior people and they assimilate when they have opportunity. We need them industrially more than they need us. They need the gospel and it is ours to give.

Opposition Only in a Narrow Range

The causes of the exclusion and singular treatment of Chinese and Japanese are exceptional, unjustifiable, and suicidal. The real builders of the West and the Christian forces there have no more sympathy with this attitude

CHINESE PASTOR AND FAMILY, PORTLAND, OREGON
CHOIR OF THE CHINESE CHURCH, SAN FRANCISCO, CALIFORNIA

American Indians and Other Peoples 215

toward Orientals than do people elsewhere. In fact they are sufferers along with these immigrants, as they are in sore need of their service.

We touch elsewhere on the strategic importance of home missions among these people. Close contact with these Christians disarms all prejudice. Their fidelity, fervency, and self-sacrifice challenge the best that is in us. They prompt us to a higher plane of spiritual life and service. They are strangers here and should see reflected in us the face of Jesus Christ. These missions have resulted in strong reenforcements to the foreign fields. *(Close Contact Disarms Prejudice)*

Chinese Christians in one denomination in this country, at their own initiative and expense, opened and maintain a Christian mission in China. When we consider the future of Japan and China as related to the coming kingdom, is it not providential that on our own shores we may so deal with our Eastern brothers as to produce results more far-reaching than with the same number in China itself? Is not a fair gage of how much we care about saving our brother across the sea, the interest we take in him when he is here? *(Influences Reaching Over Sea)*

QUESTIONS ON CHAPTER VI

AIM: TO REALIZE THE OPPORTUNITY FOR CHRISTIAN EFFORT AMONG THE AMERICAN INDIANS, MEXICANS, JAPANESE, AND CHINESE

I. *The American Indians.*

1.* By what right did our forefathers settle in America?
2. To whom did the country belong?
3. Were the Indians making the most of their resources?
4.* Have people from foreign lands a right to take land from others if they can accomplish more with it?
5. If the Japanese are better rice growers than Americans does that give them a right to our rice lands?
6. What constitutes the right to possession?
7. Is the law that discovery constitutes possession just to aboriginal people?
8.* Is it a Christian principle?
9. How did the early settlers get along in their relations with the Indians?
10. Name some arts that the pioneers learned from the Indians.
11. Can you name any treaties that our government made with the Indians that were violated by the Indians?

American Indians and Other Peoples

12. Can you give an example of a treaty with the Indians violated by our government?

13.* By what right did our government place the Indians on reservations?

14. How does the land on which the Indians are located compare in productiveness with that which they once held?

15. Is it possible for the Indians to make a living on these reservations?

16. How have the reservations proved an injury to the Indians?

17.* Can a good type of manhood and womanhood be developed in laziness?

18. What do you consider the best adjustment to be made with the Indians in view of our past injustice to them?

19. Do the Indians need Christianity?

20. Are the Indians ready to receive gospel teaching?

21. Can you give any examples of good, earnest Indian Christians?

22. Where are most of the Indians now located?

23. How many missionaries has your board among them?

24.* Do you believe that under the new Indian policy the opportunity for successful mission work has been increased? Give reasons.

II. *The Mexicans.*

25. How many Mexicans are there under our flag?

26. What are their chief temptations?

27. What type of mission work is most successful among them?

28. Has your mission board work among them?

III. *The Japanese.*

29. Have the Japanese proved themselves equal to the Americans in commercial activity?

30. Why do the Japanese come to the United States?

31. What type of people come?

32. Do you know of any foreigners who adopt American customs more readily?

33. What is their Oriental religious faith?

34. What kind of Christians do they become?

35.* How will Christianizing them in America aid both home and foreign missions?

IV. *The Chinese.*

36. Do you believe that the Chinese may some day become our strongest commercial rivals?

37. Has our treatment of the Chinese in this country been such as we should feel was just for us in their country?

38. Has our treatment of them aided missionary work among them?

39. In view of this, how do you account for the success of missions among them?

40. Sum up as strongly as possible the importance of mission work among the Chinese.

REFERENCES FOR FURTHER STUDY

CHAPTER VI

I. *Indians.*

Forbes-Lindsay: "Shaping the Future of the Indians." World To-day, March, '07.
Humphrey: The Indian Dispossessed, I-III.
Johnston: Indian and Spanish Neighbors, I-III.
Kennan: "Lands of Indians and Fair Play." Outlook, February 27, '04.
Leupp: "Gospel of Work for Indians." Nation, October 6, '04.
McBeth: The Nez Perces Since Lewis and Clark, XVII, XVIII.
Oskison: "Making an Individual of the Indian." Everybody's Magazine, June, '07.
Oskison: "Remaining Causes of Indian Discontent." North American Review, March 1, '07.
Riggin: in Methodism and the Republic, 299-308.

II. *Japanese in the United States.*

Fulton: "Japanese Pupils in American Schools." North American Review, December, '06.
Inglis: "Reasons for California's Attitude Toward the Japanese." Harper's Weekly, January 19, '07.
Johnson: in Methodism and the Republic, 194-213.
Kawakami: "The Japanese in California." Independent, November 29, '06.

Kawakami: "Naturalization of the Japanese." North American Review, June, '07.

Thompson: "Japanese in San Francisco." World To-day, December, '06.

III. *Chinese in the United States.*

Harwood: "Extinction of the Chinese in the United States." World's Work, December, '04.

Irwin: "Chinese Slave Trade in California." Everybody's Magazine, July, '04.

James: in Methodism and the Republic, 171-193.

Nickerson: "Chinese Treaties and Legislation of the United States and their Enforcement." North American Review, September, '05.

THE WEST AND THE EAST

This North American continent is a laboratory of grace. How graciously shall the nations be graced by its grace? Men and continents are saved to serve. Only a saved life can render an effective saving service. A wise purpose has chosen this continent and visited it with supremely benign favors. May God vindicate, through the continent's pure ministry to the world, the wisdom of his own choice. May God grant that we, his colaborers, shall vindicate the wisdom of that choice.
—*McAfee*

The Christian young people of the American Churches have had deposited with them a great trust. "Who say ye that I am?" the Master seems ever to be asking all his twentieth century disciples. By holding his exalted ideas fixedly before us; by generous gifts for the widening of his kingdom; by devotedness to present duty as he reveals it to us, we shall answer this supreme question so clearly that all about us may hear. If by our conduct we make winsome the gospel and the life of the Son of God; if we conscientiously use our means as Christian stewards, giving with a clear conscience up to the limit of our ability, then we shall with cheer and courage hasten the coming of the Master's kingdom in America, that America, Christianized, may use to the utmost her unequaled opportunity for the evangelization of the world.
—*Shelton*

VII

THE WEST AND THE EAST

Suppose we climb a mountain and from the outlook trace the way we have come. We recount the mile-stones marking our highway of national destiny. *(Counting the Mile-Stones)*

We again note our country's providential location and the divine plan in its physical features. We scan explorers' paths and find their ways opened or closed as they helped or hindered an overshadowing purpose. We watch the awakening of the arid West and mark the quickened currents of life in the Northwest, the West, the Southwest. Everywhere we find multitudes gathering and titanic forces operating. But all paths and rivers and railways like veins and arteries carry our life streams oceanward; and, there flowing as they may, they all eventually unite in a resistless ocean tide Orientward. *(The Destined Goal)*

Our Internal Development

Our internal material development we observe is threefold. First is *the railroad*. In *(Railroads)* the earlier days the crawling "prairie schooner" or the few trains on solitary railways, carrying people to favored oases of the trans-Mississippi country, caused little congestion of populations, and that at so comparatively slow a rate as to enable the Church to make adjustments with something like deliberateness. Now the West is becoming a net of railways. Great trunk lines multiply in all directions. Thousands of people are emptied on wide areas in a single month. The situation changes as by magic. The old order of pioneering is as inadequate and out of date as are former facilities for travel. The Church will never overtake this swiftly-moving, swarming West with ox-team and schooner.

Opening Up of New Territory

Another factor is *the opening up of new territory*. Take Oklahoma and other broad reservations thrown open to settlers, who camped on their borders like locusts, waiting for the entrance shot to be fired. Improvised towns spring up in a single night, and improvements on a broad scale and of enduring nature follow with astounding rapidity. Church privileges are wholly inadequate for multitudes who never needed them anything like as now, while at the same time the forces of evil are multiplied in number and hold the lead, playing with deadly execution upon the laxened moral life of the community. The evil one pickets new settlements with cavalry and machine guns. The Church can hardly expect to capture the situation with a few poorly provisioned, brave scouts armed with muskets of '61.

Another element is *irrigation*. Hundreds of square miles marked "desert" are changed to acres of amazing fertility; and this good work continues. The government wisely expends millions upon millions in reclaiming "bad lands." Where the early pioneer picked his way among sagebrush and arid desolation is now landscape billowing with plenty and beautiful with orchards of luscious fruits; and this is but a beginning. That is no place to bring the water of life in sickly, drying rivulets.

Irrigation

An Urgent Crisis

Do not misunderstand us. We do not discount the splendid strategic work the Church has done in the West. Our meaning is, such quick and unprecedented changes are now taking place in these regions, and on a scale so stupendous, that opportunities may completely

Adequate Response

distance us before we of the East awake to the new conditions. Whatever is done there, if effective, must, like other enterprises, be characterized by alertness, push, statesmanship, and cash. Men without means and missionary enterprises with meager appropriations find the situation too large for little undertakings.

Men of Exploits

Yet we have never had more able leaders, more heroic, self-denying preachers, or those who have won larger victories in proportion to the munitions supplied than these splendid men of the frontier: young men from our colleges who scorn easier tasks and clerical emoluments; men of exploits who prefer, and on short rations if they must, to carve empires out of the wilderness rather than to stand as they might in stately churches and minister to complacent congregations.

Tense and Tremendous Situations

Concerning the whole home missionary situation, one who reads reports coming from any part of the West encounters appeals for immediate relief of tense and tremendous situations, and hardly knows which is the most pressing. If the scope of this book covered the South, New England, and the Cities, the same heart-breaking urgency would, in various forms, be reflected from every quarter.

The flood is already submerging the missionary boards, but it is nothing to what it may become in three years. The truth is, we have never known anything like the present stress in home missionary enterprises. It is all so sudden that few pastors even understand about it. Our greatest peril is the ignorance of the Churches generally upon the whole subject; yet, the new tide that rises will not wait for us leisurely to face the situation. The emergency is unprecedented. It cannot be at all met in the West by present forces and present missionary contributions. We will here and there find a quiet eddy which may lead some to question extreme conditions as depicted; yet whoever covers the field with a wide sweep of observation is shut up to but one conclusion.

Need of Enlightenment

Wide Meaning of Movements

It is evident to any who give the matter thought that the foreign field likewise demands a general and positive reenforcement. The West has the needed latent resources of every kind. It is clear that the older parts of our country will not alone furnish for the foreign field what is instant and imperative. An extension of our base of supplies is essential. For

Reflex Results for Foreign Field

the missionary forces of the Church to invest largely in the West is literally to reclaim an empire whose revenues, spiritual and material, will in five years begin flowing into missionary treasuries, and with such rising liberality as to dwarf all preliminary expenditures. Have we not come to a time when we must, of necessity, arise and save our own land if humanity is to be saved? America for Christ means the world for Christ, but the *whole round world* for Christ means *all* America as his.

Wise Beginnings

It is providential that beginnings were made and the work strenuously advanced before the larger purpose of God was manifested. It now appears that not a church has been built and not a missionary enlisted without directly contributing to an all-inclusive plan.

Importance of Early Aid

One board in forty years has aided in the erection of fifteen thousand churches, more than half of them west of the Mississippi. When the Louisiana Purchase became a part of the United States it had but 522 churches in all its borders, and now this one denomination has seven thousand churches there, six thousand of which were aided by missionary funds. How hopeless would seem the task in our West to-day if Protestantism

PLYMOUTH CONGREGATIONAL CHURCH, SEATTLE, WASHINGTON

MEXICAN HOME MISSION BAPTIST CHURCH, EL PASO, TEXAS

all these years had not steadily extended her borders. These many churches there are now our battle-line for the greatest advance of the ages. Every picket detachment will be swelled to a company and every company to a regiment. The Church, when it knows, will not hesitate. The rising emergency will be overtopped by wide-spread enthusiastic enlistment.

When Christ was born his Church was poor and few in numbers. Wise men of the East brought gifts to him. Now since he has been lifted up he is drawing all men unto him, and his Church has tens of thousands for recruits and untold millions of gold to fill his treasury. Surely when he is in the field, when he unrolls for us his map of imperial purpose, every one of us will count it honor and joy to say, "Lord, what wilt thou have me to do?" *Christ's Imperial Purpose*

The Church's Education Concerning Home Missions

It is evident that a first move in fully reclaiming the West is to get before the whole Church the present status of the frontier. It is safe to say that our country west of the Mississippi is, in its missionary conditions and *Knowledge Needed of Present Frontier* possibilities, not so well known by the Church generally as is India. Missionary education has been largely concerning the foreign field. This is fortunate, for with our natural tendency to greater interest in home rather than in foreign affairs, had the home field been most exploited in literature and public utterance, it would now be more difficult to arouse an adequate interest in the foreign work.

Foreign Field Has Preoccupied Attention

While home missions are in the heart of the Church, yet the divine plan has been so unmistakable concerning the Church among the nations, and the succession of notable victories there has been so marked and far-reaching, as largely to preoccupy the attention of Christendom.

Home Field Now to the Front

A rapid change of front in the United States is so recent as to attract the attention of the observant only. Not that forces on the foreign field are now less aggressive or successful, but that in addition the home field presents such a massing of multitudes and such wide-spread significant preparations as to indicate a culmination beyond anything in American religious history.

Preparation for a World Movement

As we have endeavored to show in preceding chapters, God seems to be calling out large reenforcements and training them for a world movement. The West suddenly awakens as if answering a divine summons, and developments of every kind go forward as if responding to imperial urgency. America is none too large for these evolutions of the armies of the Lord.

Fragmentary Literature — Concerning this newer situation, little literature save of a fragmentary kind exists. Missionary boards have furnished periodical sketches and leaflets, and doubtless within the next year they will send out much more on the new West.

Campaign for Fresh Information — This information, however, reaches but a part of the Church; hence a very urgent service needed is what all may render, namely, to secure from your board its newest home missionary literature and circulate it in your local church. So far as you are concerned the greatest home missionary field, next to yourself, is the church where you worship. The reason is evident. The chief obstacles to missionary advance at home and abroad are not the peoples to be evangelized, languages to be learned, or hardships to be endured; all doors are wide open, save one, and that is the one into the individual church, out of which must largely come missionary support and the missionaries themselves. It has been aptly said: "There have been no failures in foreign missions anywhere except in some of our churches at home."

Selfishness Hardest to Overcome

We can change the cannibals in the Fiji Islands and make them so far Christian that a woman to-day can go in safety from one end of the islands to the other unattended. We can change the high-class Brahman so that an invalid outcast whom he would not look at a few years ago he is now willing to sit up all night with and feed with a spoon. All this foreign mission work has done and can continue to do. What it has not yet done here in the homeland is to change the selfishness of our own people into a spirit of sacrificial interest for the saving of the world.

Low Percentage of Missionary Gifts

While our Church-members give, on the average, only two cents a week to save the millions for whom we are responsible, we have little to boast of. Contrast this with the generosity of Christians across the sea. The native Zulu Christians have taken the full support of all their own churches and are contributing money to send the gospel to others. At the time of the famine in India, when the native Christians were paid out of the general fund twenty cents a week for their support, they insisted on giving ten per cent. of it back again to the missionaries for Church work. There is a native Christian pastor in China, formerly a gambler, with a large family and a salary of fifty dollars a year, who gives twenty per cent. of it for missionary work. These men are not exceptions; they represent the sacrifices which native Christians are ready to make. It is good generalship to strengthen ourselves at the weakest point.

We need pastors here at home with a passion for missions. It is a material age. Our people, as a whole, love ease and luxury; we want everything for ourselves first, and we need pastors more than ever who will have the courage to preach to us in no uncertain terms about Christian stewardship. We want ministers who will not be afraid to tell the people in the pews that the money they have is not their own, but it is God's money which they hold in trust; and that the question, when the claim of missions is presented, is not, "How much of our money will we give to the Lord?" but rather, "How much of the Lord's money are we going to keep for ourselves?"[1] A business man told

Pastors Must Have a Passion for Missions

---
[1] S. B. Capen.

why he increased his missionary offering during a financial panic. He said the boards had more pressing calls for funds then, also that many would likely shrink in their missionary contributions. But as such times call for special self-sacrifice and heroism, he thought a still larger number might increase their offerings and thus give the boards the larger emergency funds needed.

Appeal of the Multitude

An intelligent, well-directed campaign of information and prayer concerning the present missionary situation in the United States will bring larger results for every field than any other means. Missionary treasuries are replenished by the many. The alabaster box and the widow's mite are among the chief assets of the Church militant. Who goes straight to the people with the story of the waiting multitudes will find a ready and generous response. That story brings to God's people reminders of the ever-present Christ and his compassion for the multitudes, and again in your message they will hear him say, "Give ye them to eat." For the people to place in the hands of Jesus their loaves and fishes and thereby, with his blessing, satisfy the hunger of millions, is no more vital to others than to themselves. They thus feed themselves; for are not twelve baskets full more than five loaves?

Use of the Highest Motives

Obedience to the missionary commission is fundamental to the life of the Church. That life is born in self-surrender. It unfolds and matures in Christlike service. No Church can escape a choice between two fields—a missionary field or a cemetery. The statement is ever new, "My people perish for lack of knowledge." <small>Obeying the Commission</small>

The story of the world's need told to your church, and presented in its various organizations, is as essential to their spiritual life as is the gospel of Christ to the heathen for their salvation. You cannot possibly otherwise so vitalize the missionary movement as prayerfully to advertise its needs. When you are filled with information a new dynamo will be turned on. You have the essentials: intelligence, sources of information, and the gift of utterance. When these are brought to bear on your church it will respond, for as a rule God's people do not withhold their gifts when they hear his voice. <small>Story of the World's Needs</small>

The motive, after all, which must move the Church, is not proportionate giving or system- <small>Divine Self-Investment</small>

atic giving. It is not incited by mere duty or the needs of others. These are all important and would be sufficient if there were not a greater; but overshadowing and including all these is the desire and direct command of Jesus, "As the Father hath sent me, even so send I you." This command is personal and complete. In one way or another we are asked to invest self. The nature and extent of that investment is seen in the manner God sent Jesus into the world. Note the "as" and "so" of the commandment. The second equals the first.

Power of Love and the Cross

God had one Son. He loved him. He also loved the world. He could not rescue the world and withhold his Son. He offered up the One that he might have both. The mind of the Son was that of the Father. The sending of Jesus into the world cost him poverty, persecution, agony, and crucifixion. These facts did not indicate less of God's love for the Son, but they help us to measure the love of the Father and the Son for a lost world. And after all, it is the cross that draws men Godward. The man Jesus gripped the world by renouncing it. He saved his life by losing it. No one ever so obliterated himself for the world, and the world has never so enshrined another.

Christ is King of kings because he is servant of servants. His utter humiliation is the measure of his exaltation. Now we are God's commissioned ones to continue and complete the work of Jesus. We are "sent" "as" Jesus was sent by the Father. He invests us with the same program of renunciation and the same promise of victory. The two are inseparable. The world bows to the kingship of great souls in proportion as they have exemplified this command of Jesus. *Impelling Effect of Christ's Example*

Christ's lordship and ownership are gospel notes we must sound out clear and often. We enthrone him nowhere only as we enthrone him within. If he reigns in us, then he reigns through us; and whatever we have is his to that end. Christ is not an absentee owner. He takes complete direction of your life for himself. Christian stewardship—or the lack of it—stands more in the way of Christ's advance than all the obstacles of the heathen world. Consecrated treasure means a consecrated Church, "For where your treasure is, there will your heart be also." The heathen of this and all other continents will not withstand an advance of that kind. Does the Church acknowledge the present direction and *Lordship and Ownership*

ownership of Christ? Do the average payments of its members for missionary conquest indicate this?

Obedience Measures Power

The Attitude for World Conquest

The measure of power in yourself or in your local church is the measure of obedience to this command. We can no more have a church apart from this marching order than we can have Christianity without Christ. Obedience to this commission is not a matter of geography but of surrender. Attitude determines longitude. The apostolic Church waited for the promise in an attitude of self-abandonment. The command was "beginning at Jerusalem." It was the hardest place in which to begin and to prevail. Nowhere was the tide so against the Church, but if they might receive power to overcome Jerusalem, the rest of the world was as good as vanquished. An enduement that would win Jerusalem would work anywhere. This is the secret of an overcoming Christianity—the kind that can win at our Jerusalem: that is, in our life, our church, our country. In that apostolic Church the ultimate aim was world conquest, but the test of its equipment was its power in Jerusalem. In that attitude they prayed and waited, and for that purpose the Spirit was imparted. The tongues of fire which burned their way to the ends of the earth blazed a pathway by the way of Jerusalem. That spirit in your life and in your study class will work the same wonders in your local church. By way of it and our homeland, the gospel will gladden "every creature." The answer to the local problems of individual churches is their right answer to Christ's missionary commandment.

How would you estimate a professing Christian or a church that ignored the decalogue, in whole or in part? Is this missionary law less binding? We dwell at some length on this as the whole issue centers here. All attempted substitutes are puerile and confusing. If Christ had substituted anything for Calvary this would not be a missionary era. *(The Missionary Law Comes from Calvary)*

When you give yourself, the gospel dispensation dominates your life. You become conscious of spiritual illumination and rest of soul. Christ in his surrender spake concerning his illumination; not only was he glad "for the joy that was set before him" but he thereby discovered the secret of human living. He says, "Take my yoke upon you, and learn of me; for *(Secret of Soul Rest)*

I am meek and lowly in heart: and ye shall find rest unto your souls." He tells the secret. It is a yoke of service, but it will prove an easy one if we learn from him how to wear it. Meekness and lowliness of heart—self-renunciation—mean soul rest.

Christ Revealed

Then again this attitude is what reveals Christ to us. He says, Go everywhere, tell the good news to every creature, *"and lo, I am with you always."* Is this preaching? Possibly, but are not these truths translated into the life of the Church the beginning and end of all missionary effort?

Suggestive Methods

And now in what other ways may the local church be helped to answer the Master's call?

Monthly Missionary Prayer-meeting

The monthly missionary prayer-meeting gives tone to the membership. Many may not attend, and the beginnings may not tingle with enthusiasm, but, when your purpose is announced, a number will be thankful that they are to meet in the regular prayer-meeting once a month and talk and pray about Christ's world conquest. You will be surprised to find just who are interested. Among them may be a number of quiet people whose missionary interest you had not discovered. However, the Lord who sits over against the treasury has known. The Christ, always present with those who according to the commandment go to the ends of the earth, also meets with these who gather to inquire about his purpose. As they travel in prayer to needy fields, Jesus himself draws near, and their hearts, like those of the disciples of old, burn within them.

We cite as an example, a down-town church where conditions of success might be counted doubtful. It is a congregation of the people with fluctuating membership. The gospel of world salvation and Christian stewardship, the missionary prayer service, the mission study classes, each in proper season and with no attempt at undue prominence, are made a part of the regular calendar. *A Practical Calendar*

No one contributes largely from his plenty, but the many, gladly and without pressure, give as unto God, and the total is a surprise to all. Financial ability falls far below that of other congregations, but in missionary offerings these people lead all the churches of that denomination in a large city. Its own treasury does not lack. There are no deficits. Penitents seeking pardon and wanderers returning to God find *Without Friction and Without Deficits* this church a convenient and attractive gateway to the Father's house. This is but one example of scores.

Training the Sunday-school

Then there is your Sunday-school. The redemption of America and beyond must largely come by way of those now in our Sunday-schools. The teacher is the diamond pivot on which a door may swing and the outstreaming light flood uneven pathways.

Missionary Teachers and Committees

Is method important? Yes, but the spirit is everything. A Sunday-school teacher may again and again go to the mission field in the persons of those who hear God's call in the faithful teaching and holy living. The committee in charge of monthly missionary exercises in the Sunday-school are the King's recruiting-officers. They will exercise great care that their offices and their programs are not perfunctory.

Mission Study Class

That study class may be waiting your initiative. You cannot? Read the prophets—their hesitation, their fear; but God called, and retreat meant disaster. God wins most of his victories through people like yourself. To refuse is our unmaking. Only the one-talent man failed. He did not try. "Seek ye first the kingdom of God." Aim that it stand *first*. If in

The West and the East

your young people's society it is not where it should be, help to push it up to first place. *seek* to place it there. Study over it, pray, consult, work, persevere, be bound to find a way and Christ will *make* a way.

No excuses may we offer for failure. Too much is at stake. You will not excuse a missionary who deserts his field; you cannot. You listen to his tale of hardship, and yet feel he should have stayed. Does God call him to stay more than he calls us to provide conditions that make staying less difficult? Can you turn from that study class, that Sunday-school, that hard task, because it is *hard,* even bordering on the impossible? Has not God as truly placed us just where we are faithfully to perform our task, and that if need be at as great cost as if in a mission field? Does he call a number to go and win, and excuse us if we fail at home?

No Excuse Acceptable

The Missionaries and the Home Field

The home field and the local church just now are where the tide of battle centers. Missionaries, home and foreign, prayerfully watch the outcome. As we value destiny we dare not fail. God has entrusted to us the responsibilities of this crucial hour.

Sacred Responsibility

Forces at the Front

And, after all, who are these people at the front, these missionaries scattered over the waste places of this republic? Do we wonder what it is to see with their eyes stubborn conditions in the midst of which they toil? They are flesh and blood, people of like passions with ourselves. Are we asking if the battle goes hard against them, and if the load at times seems unbearable?

Deserve to be Sustained

Do they sometimes ask why they enlisted in such warfare? Why they should serve with rigor, and live on a pittance, and away from friends and scenes that clutch at their heart when they dare think of them? Are they tempted with the thought that the Church too much forgets? Does it seem to them that, when they have sacrificed so much, the Church should not tie their hands with lack of support for the work?

Reflecting the Master

Brave souls—choice spirits of the Church militant, they utter no complaint, nor does censure fall from their patient lips. We see in them an incarnation that suggests the Master. They are Christian evidences in shoes. They, on the altar of self-surrender, break an alabaster box that fills all the Church with a sweet odor of holy living and high service. While they continue we cannot lose the heavenly vision.

Personal Consideration

Look Not for Substitutes

One danger if avoided may save the Church a wealth of possibilities in these ripening fields. That danger is the thought that if you, your class, your young people's society, or church does not take up some particular work mentioned, another will do it. That spirit predominant means disaster. Do what you can— and do it now! Take facts presented, counsel with others about them, write your board or the superintendent of the mission to which your heart turns, for further particulars if needed, and your example, multiplied by many, may mean a hastened millennium for whole regions that otherwise may too long continue as they are. If you are not to help, who should?

Look at the Need

Better still, what do the young men and women of the Church propose to do with such a call, for instance, as comes to a single board from Oklahoma and other points? Twenty men needed—not anybody, but as good as the Church furnishes. Bright, stalwart fellows just graduated from theological schools, or men of experience. If God does not in such an emergency call you, then to whom is the appeal directed?

Frontier Work a Keen Test

Frontiers, once enchanting fiction, are now bleak prose. The romance of missions is born of remoteness. The Christian's highest consecration may now mean, not a distant heathen land, but the one slipped under his feet. His battle may be not so much to go, as to stay. It is his Bunker Hill or Waterloo.

Enlistment of a New Brotherhood

Suppose a new order of brotherhood were inaugurated—a band of men to work where others do not care to go—men to get under the load, to stay there until God calls them elsewhere. We mean an exact duplication of foreign missionary zeal expended on American soil. That spirit will work resurrection. It will beget a like consecration. Evil spirits will flee before it. Let us not be misunderstood; this is not even an implied reflection on modern preachers. As a whole, they represent a loyalty to Christ unsurpassed, unless it be by preachers' wives. We refer to a new enlistment for special service.

Challenge of an Emergency

In a national emergency, citizens thrust aside ordinary considerations to render extraordinary service. The kingdom of God in the United States is in instant need of the surren-

BAPTIST WHITE TEMPLE, OKLAHOMA CITY, OKLAHOMA

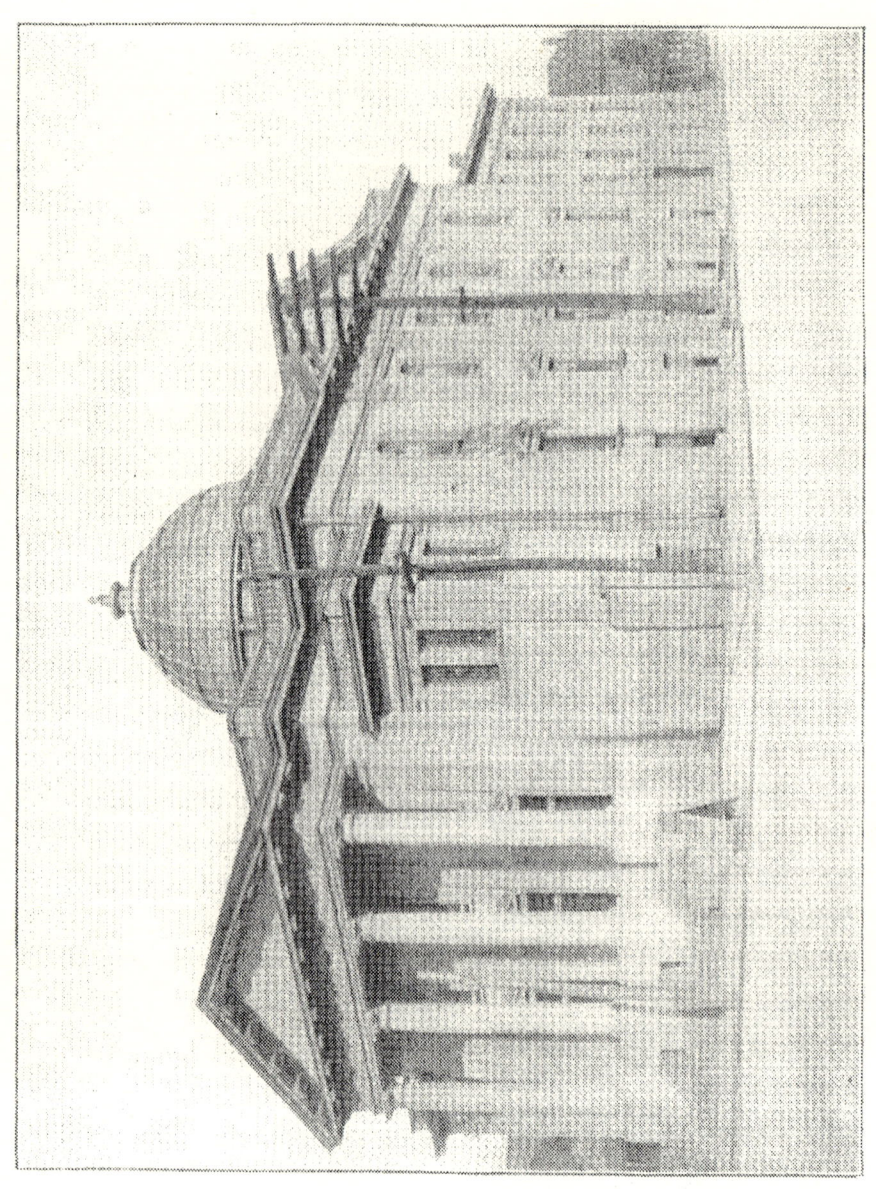

dered treasure and toil of its subjects. A campaign of redemption of waste places cannot succeed by proxy or absent treatment. There is no redemption without the shedding of blood. We mean, there can be adequate returns only on investments that cost what is as dear as life. Christ himself thought it not worth while to make any attempt to save men on a cheaper basis—*he gave himself.*

Humanly speaking the man is everything. Put him anywhere, and what ought to be, happens. Is any one too good to go? Was Abraham or Paul or the Man of Nazareth too valuable a man to undertake a mission? With such heroic opportunities facing him, no young man in the ministry need be long in deciding whether he will go where most needed or stay where least self-denial is required. All sentimentality about high purpose and lofty consecration shrivels in the noonday light of unanswered, momentous obligations. The Christian man who does not squarely face the responsibility, it may be of going, certainly of sending, may well ask himself to what purpose he lives and whom he serves. *It Comes to the Individual Man*

Young man, this is for you. If you will invest in what is worth while, consecrate your- *Bugle-Call to the Young Men* self to a Christlike lay service in any Christless locality, or, if God calls you, enter the ministry just as you would the missionary field. Fling to the winds anxiety about pastorates, rank, preferment, and so-called ministerial success. By prayer and a close walk with God maintain that spirit to the close of your ministry. When you become self-conscious you are a dead preacher.

<small>The Young Women Summoned</small>

Young woman, you may be the one for whom that mining camp is waiting. That may be your call. Do you say you are so busy in your home church you cannot well be spared? If you can be easily spared you may not be wanted. Is not this call, "America for Christ," becoming personal?

<small>A Standard for Young People</small>

This enlistment for service in any place by young people who come to the work exactly as they would go to the foreign field will do for home missions in the United States what Christ asks. Young people, "Whatsoever he saith unto you, do it."

<small>Immortal Hebrew Names</small>

We might never have heard of Abraham or Paul had they refused their westward call. It was their making and their crown of immortality. In the rapid expansion of the kingdom in apostolic days, in the doors then thrown wide, and in victories all out of proportion to those engaged, we recognize the omnipotent, omnipresent, unconquerable Christ. One fact alone bewilders. Israel—blind, unresponsive, inscrutable Israel!

God hath raised up another Israel. We face an epoch. Is he not saying, "Arise, shine; for thy light is come, and the glory of Jehovah is risen upon thee"? And thus may our West gain help from our East, that in turn it may bear "the glory of Jehovah" to the waiting Orient.

Mission of a New Israel

QUESTIONS ON CHAPTER VII

AIM: TO REALIZE WHAT EACH ONE MAY DO TO INCREASE THE MISSIONARY INTEREST IN HIS LOCAL CHURCH

1. What needs on the frontier have impressed you most?
2. Name some new impressions that you have received in this study.
3. Compare the area of the territory west of the Mississippi with that east of the Mississippi.
4. Compare the population west of the Mississippi with that east of the Mississippi.
5. Give some examples of how railroads have contributed to the development of the country.
6. Could the interior country be developed without them?

7. Sum up the effect of irrigation on the work of home missions.
8. State all the reasons you can why the Church should quickly occupy the frontier.
9. Can the Churches gain anything by postponing activity?
10. Sum up the loss that will come to the Church from delay.
11. What would you suggest to be done in your own young people's society to acquaint the members with the needs on the frontier?
12. How can you acquaint the Sunday-school with these facts?
13. How can you educate your church through the weekly prayer-meetings regarding these pressing needs on the frontier?
14. Do you believe that your church is familiar with these conditions?
15. How much has your church increased its gifts to home missions during the past three years?
16. Why do Church-members not give more to work outside of their own parishes?
17. Is it because of a lack of vision or consecration?
18. What do you consider the main cause for a lack of gifts to home missions?
19. Why is it that people won from heathenism and paganism are more generous in their gifts according to their resources than we at home?
20. Do you suppose that prayer for missions would stimulate giving?

The West and the East

21. How often does your church hold missionary prayer-meetings?
22.* Name what to you are the highest motives for missionary work.
23. Do these motives depend largely upon your own Christian experience?
24. Would you say that persons who have little interest in missions have a meager knowledge of the real blessings of Christ?
25. Is it possible to crown Christ King of our lives and yet not have a deep interest in missions?
26. Do you suppose a missionary could be successful without a consecrated life?
27. Why does he become a missionary?
28. Is there any power in his life which should not be in yours?
29. What can you do to increase the missionary spirit in your church?
30. Have you ever thought of becoming a missionary?

REFERENCES FOR FURTHER STUDY
CHAPTER VII

For further material on this chapter the Secretary in charge of mission study of your denominational board should be addressed.

APPENDIXES

APPENDIX A

TABLE SHOWING ORIGINAL TERRITORY AND ADDITIONS TO THE UNITED STATES IN AREA AND POPULATION [1]

Territory	Area in Square Miles	Population When Acquired	Population in 1900	Present Division into States and Territories
Original Territory	About 820,000	About 4,000,000	About 51,000,000	Ala., Conn., Del., D. C., Ga., Ill., Ind., Ky., Me., Md., Mass., Mich., N. H., N. J., N. Y., N. C., O., Pa., R. I., S. C., Tenn., Vt., Va., W. Va., Wis.
Province of Louisiana, 1803	About 900,000	75,000	About 16,000,000	Ark., Cal., N.Dak., Ind. Ter., Iowa, Kans., La., Minn., Mo., Mont., Neb., Okla., S. Dak., Wyo.
Florida, 1819	66,612	About 5,000	About 500,000	Florida and small parts of Ala., La., and Miss.
Texas, 1845	376,133	About 150,000	About 3,000,000	Texas and parts of Col., Kan., N. M., and Okla.
Oregon Country, 1846	288,345	About 10,000	About 1,200,000	Idaho, Wash., Oregon, and parts of Mont. and Wyo.
New Mexico and California, 1848; Gadsden Purchase, 1853	About 590,000	About 75,000	About 2,000,000	Ariz., Cal., Nev., Utah, and parts of Cal., N.M., and Wyo.

[1] Mowry, *Territorial Growth of the United States*, 225.

APPENDIX B

LAND AREA, POPULATION, AND DENSITY OF POPULATION FOR 1900 AND 1906, BY STATES AND TERRITORIES [1]

State or Territory	Area in Square Miles	Population 1900	Estimated Population 1906	Persons per Sq Mile 1900	Persons per Sq Mile 1906
Alabama	51,998	1,828,697	2,017,877	36	39
Arizona	113,956	122,931	143,745	1	1
Arkansas	53,335	1,311,564	1,421,574	25	27
California	158,297	1,485,053	1,648,049	10	11
Colorado	103,948	539,700	615,570	5	6
Connecticut	4,965	908,420	1,005,716	188	209
Delaware	2,370	184,735	194,479	94	99
District of Columbia	70	278,718	307,716	4,645	5,129
Florida	58,666	528,542	629,341	10	11
Georgia	59,265	2,216,331	2,443,719	38	42
Idaho	84,313	161,772	205,704	2	2
Illinois	56,665	4,821,550	5,418,670	86	97
Indian Territory	31,209	392,060	519,188	13	17
Indiana	36,354	2,516,462	2,710,898	70	76
Iowa	56,147	2,231,853	2,205,690	40	40
Kansas	82,158	1,470,495	[2] 1,612,471	18	20
Kentucky	40,598	2,147,174	2,320,298	54	58
Louisiana	48,506	1,381,625	1,539,449	30	34
Maine	33,040	694,466	714,494	23	24
Maryland	12,327	1,188,044	1,275,434	121	128
Massachusetts	8,266	2,805,346	3,043,346	349	379
Michigan	57,980	2,420,982	2,584,533	42	45
Minnesota	84,682	1,751,394	2,025,615	22	25
Mississippi	46,865	1,551,270	1,708,272	34	37
Missouri	69,420	3,106,655	3,363,153	45	49
Montana	146,572	243,329	303,575	2	2
Nebraska	77,520	1,066,300	1,068,484	14	14
Nevada [3]	110,690	42,335	42,335	([4])	([4])
New Hampshire	9,341	411,588	432,624	46	48
New Jersey	8,224	1,883,669	2,196,237	250	292
New Mexico	122,634	195,310	216,328	2	2
New York	49,204	7,268,894	8,226,990	153	173
North Carolina	52,426	1,893,810	2,059,326	39	42
North Dakota	70,837	319,146	463,784	5	7
Ohio	41,040	4,157,545	4,448,677	102	109
Oklahoma	38,848	398,331	590,247	10	15
Oregon	96,699	413,536	474,738	4	5
Pennsylvania	45,126	6,302,115	6,928,515	140	155
Rhode Island	1,248	428,556	490,387	407	460
South Carolina	30,989	1,340,316	1,453,818	44	48
South Dakota	77,615	401,570	465,908	5	6
Tennessee	42,022	2,020,616	2,172,476	48	52
Texas	265,896	3,048,710	3,536,618	12	13
Utah	84,990	276,749	316,331	3	4
Vermont	9,564	343,641	350,373	38	38
Virginia	42,627	1,854,184	1,973,104	46	49
Washington	69,127	518,103	614,625	8	9
West Virginia	24,170	958,800	1,076,406	39	45
Wisconsin	56,066	2,069,042	2,260,930	38	41
Wyoming	97,914	92,531	103,673	1	1
Total for Continental United States	3,026,789	75,994,575	83,941,510	26	28

[1] Bureau of the Census, Bulletin 71, p. 16. [2] State census.
[3] Population decreased from 1890 to 1900; has increased since that date, but no reliable data to show increase; population in 1900 used instead of estimates. [4] Less than one person per square mile.

APPENDIX C

VACANT AND RESERVED AREAS IN THE WESTERN PUBLIC LAND STATES [1]

State or Territory	Total Area Acres	Vacant Acres	Per Cent.	Reserved Acres	Per Cent.
Arizona	72,332,800	47,082,321	65.1	20,344,487	28.1
California	101,350,400	33,156,877	32.7	21,874,865	21.6
Colorado	66,512,000	30,110,586	45.3	11,197,552	16.8
Idaho	53,272,000	33,485,389	62.9	7,801,355	14.4
Kansas	52,531,200	942,483	1.8	120,215	0.2
Montana	93,491,200	55,748,400	59.6	18,566,188	19.9
Nebraska	49,606,400	4,481,958	9.0	628,855	1.3
Nevada	70,848,000	61,226,774	86.4	5,983,409	8.4
New Mexico	78,451,200	52,095,312	66.4	7,571,223	9.6
North Dakota	45,308,800	7,050,306	15.6	3,438,709	7.6
Oklahoma	24,979,200	1,983,249	7.9	1,437,117	5.8
Oregon	61,459,200	20,180,261	32.8	14,495,400	23.6
South Dakota	49,696,000	9,932,113	20.1	12,236,301	24.6
Utah	54,380,800	38,847,341	71.4	8,360,121	15.4
Washington	44,275,200	8,566,563	19.3	11,392,757	25.7
Wyoming	62,649,600	37,623,329	60.0	14,017,618	22.4
Total	981,144,000	442,513,262	45.1	159,466,172	16.2

[1] Newell, *Irrigation*, 6.

APPENDIX D
IRRIGATION PROJECTS

AREAS, COST, EXPENDITURES, ETC., ON ENTIRE PROJECTS OR SUCH UNITS AS IT IS EXPECTED TO COMPLETE BY 1911[1]

Location	Project	Area in Acres	Estimated Cost	Estimated Expenditure to December 31, 1907	Per Cent. of Completion
Arizona	Salt River	210,000	$6,300,000	$4,362,100	69.2
California	Orland	30,000	1,200,000	16,900	1.4
California—Ariz.	Yuma	100,000	4,500,000	1,876,700	41.7
Colorado	Uncompahgre	140,000	5,600,000	2,900,000	51.8
Colorado	Grand Valley	50,000	2,250,000	9,750	.4
Idaho	Minidoka	160,000	4,000,000	1,839,700	46.0
Idaho	Payette—Boise	100,000	3,000,000	1,381,500	46.5
Kansas	Garden City	8,000	350,000	282,000	80.5
Montana	Huntley	30,000	900,000	796,400	88.4
Montana	Milk River, including St. Mary	30,000	1,200,000	314,800	26.2
Montana	Sun River	16,000	500,000	344,100	69.0
Nebraska—Wyo.	North Platte	110,000	3,850,000	2,797,300	73.0
Nevada	Truckee—Carson	160,000	4,800,000	3,804,600	79.2
New Mexico	Carlsbad	20,000	640,000	579,400	81.5
New Mexico	Hondo	10,000	370,000	358,600	97.0
New Mexico	Leasburg	10,000	200,000	167,900	83.9
New Mexico—Tex.	Rio Grande	160,000	8,000,000	53,200	
North Dakota	Pumping, Buford—Trenton, Williston	40,000	1,240,000	519,600	41.9
Montana—N. Dak.	Low'r Yellowstone	66,000	2,700,000	751,850	64.9
Oregon	Umatilla	18,000	1,100,000	765,500	69.6
Oregon—California	Klamath	120,000	3,600,000	1,305,080	36.2
South Dakota	Belle Fourche	100,000	3,500,000	1,281,900	36.6
Utah	Strawberry Valley	30,000	1,500,000	418,700	27.9
Washington	Okanogan	8,000	500,000	372,180	74.4
Washington	Sunnyside	40,000	1,600,000	481,180	30.7
Washington	Tieton	24,000	1,500,000	565,420	37.6
Washington	Wapato	20,000	600,000	5,220	8.7
Wyoming	Shoshone	100,000	4,500,000	2,313,990	51.5
Total		1,910,000	$70,000,000	[2]$30,665,570	

[1] Blanchard, Statistician of United States Reclamation Service.
[2] An average of $36.65 per acre.

APPENDIX E

TEXT OF THE PRESENT IRRIGATION LAW[1]

Be it enacted by the Senate and House of Representatives of the United States of America in Congress assembled, That all moneys received from the sale and disposal of public lands in Arizona, California, Colorado, Idaho, Kansas, Montana, Nebraska, Nevada, New Mexico, North Dakota, Oklahoma, Oregon, South Dakota, Utah, Washington, and Wyoming, beginning with the fiscal year ending June thirtieth, nineteen hundred and one, including the surplus of fees and commissions in excess of allowances to registers and receivers, and excepting the five per centum of the proceeds of the sales of public lands in the above States set aside by law for educational and other purposes, shall be, and the same are hereby, reserved, set aside, and appropriated as a special fund in the Treasury to be known as the "reclamation fund," to be used in the examination and survey for and the construction and maintenance of irrigation works for the storage, diversion, and development of waters for the reclamation of arid and semiarid lands in the said States and Territories, and for the payment of all other expenditures provided for in this Act: *Provided,* that in case the receipts from the sale and disposal of public lands other than those realized from the sale and disposal of lands referred to in this section are insufficient to meet the requirements for the support of agricultural colleges in the several States and Territories, under the Act of

---
[1] Quoted from Smythe, *The Conquest of Arid America,* 344-349.

August thirtieth, eighteen hundred and ninety, entitled "An act to apply a portion of the proceeds of the public lands to the more complete endowment and support of the colleges for the benefit of agriculture and the mechanic arts, established under the provisions of an Act of Congress approved July second, eighteen hundred and sixty-two," the deficiency, if any, in the sum necessary for the support of the said colleges shall be provided for from any moneys in the Treasury not otherwise appropriated.

Sec. 2. That the Secretary of the Interior is hereby authorized and directed to make examinations and surveys for, and to locate and construct, as herein provided, irrigation works for the storage, diversion, and development of waters, including artesian wells, and to report to Congress at the beginning of each regular session as to the results of such examinations and surveys, giving estimates of cost of all contemplated works, the quantity and location of the lands which can be irrigated therefrom, and all facts relative to the practicability of each irrigation project; also the cost of works in process of construction as well as of those which have been completed.

Sec. 3. That the Secretary of the Interior shall, before giving the public notice provided for in section four of this Act, withdraw from public entry the lands required for any irrigation works contemplated under the provisions of this Act, and shall restore to public entry any of the lands so withdrawn when, in his judgment, such lands are not required for the purposes of this Act; and the Secretary of the Interior is hereby authorized, at or immediately prior to the time of beginning the surveys for any contemplated irrigation works, to withdraw from entry, except under the homestead laws, any public lands believed to be susceptible of irrigation from said works: *Provided,* That all lands entered and entries made under the homestead laws within areas so withdrawn during such withdrawal shall be subject to all the provisions, limitations, charges, terms, and conditions of this Act; that said surveys shall be prosecuted diligently to completion, and upon the completion thereof, and of the necessary maps, plans, and estimates of cost, the Secretary of the Interior shall determine whether or not said project is practicable and advisable, and if determined to be impracticable or unadvisable he shall thereupon restore said lands to entry; that public lands which it is proposed to irrigate by means of any contemplated works shall be subject to entry only under the provisions of the homestead laws in tracts of not less than forty nor more than one hundred and sixty acres, and shall be subject to the limitations, charges, terms, and conditions herein provided: *Provided,* That the commutation provisions of the homestead laws shall not apply to entries made under this Act.

Sec. 4. That upon the determination by the Secretary of the Interior that any irrigation project is practicable, he may cause to be let contracts for the construction of the same, in such portions or sections as it may be practicable to construct and complete as parts of the whole project, providing the necessary funds for such portions or sections are available in the reclamation fund, and thereupon he shall give public notice of the lands irrigable under such project, and limit of area per entry, which limit shall represent the acreage which, in the opinion of the Secretary, may be reasonably required for the support of a family upon the lands in question; also of the charges which shall be made per acre upon the said entries, and upon lands in private ownership which may be irrigated by the waters of the said irrigation project, and the number of annual instalments, not exceeding ten, in which such charges shall be paid and the time when such payments shall commence. The said charges shall be determined with a view of returning to the reclamation fund the estimated cost of construction of the project, and shall be apportioned equitably: *Provided,* That in all construction work eight hours shall constitute a day's work, and no Mongolian labor shall be employed thereon.

Sec. 5. That the entryman upon the lands to be irrigated by such works shall, in addition to compliance with the homestead laws, reclaim at least one half of the total irrigable area of his entry for agricultural purposes, and before receiving patent for the lands covered by his entry shall pay to the Government the charges apportioned against such tract, as provided in section four. No right to the use of water for land in private ownership shall be sold for a tract exceeding one hundred and sixty acres to any one landowner, and no such sale shall be made to any landowner unless he be an actual bona fide resident on such lands, or occupant thereof residing in the neighborhood of said land, and no such right shall permanently attach until all payments therefor are made. The annual instalments shall be paid to the receiver of the local land office of the district in which the land is situated, and a failure to make any two payments when due shall render the entry subject to cancelation, with the forfeiture of all rights under this Act, as well as of any moneys already paid thereon. All moneys received from the above sources shall be paid into the reclamation fund. Registers and receivers shall be allowed the usual commissions on all moneys paid for lands entered under this Act.

Sec. 6. That the Secretary of the Interior is hereby authorized and directed to use the reclamation fund for the operation and maintenance of all reservoirs and irrigation works constructed under the provisions of this Act: *Provided,* That when the payments required by this Act are made for the major portion of the lands irrigated from the waters of any of the works herein provided for, then the management and operation of such irrigation works shall pass to the owners of the lands irrigated thereby, to be maintained at their expense under such form of organization and under such rules and regulations as may be acceptable to the Secretary of the Interior: *Provided,* That the title to and the management and operation of the reservoirs and the works necessary for their protection and operation shall remain in the Government until otherwise provided by Congress.

Sec. 7. That where in carrying out the provisions of this Act it becomes necessary to acquire any rights or property, the Secretary of the Interior is hereby authorized to acquire the same for the United States by purchase or by condemnation under judicial process, and to pay from the reclamation fund the sums which may be needed for that purpose, and it shall be the duty of the Attorney-General of the United States upon every application of the Secretary of the Interior, under this Act, to cause proceedings to be commenced for condemnation within thirty days from the receipt of the application at the Department of Justice.

Sec. 8. That nothing in this Act shall be construed as affecting or intended to affect or to in any way interfere with the laws of any State or Territory relating to the control, appropriation, use, or distribution of water used in irrigation, or any vested right acquired thereunder, and the Secretary of the Interior, in carrying out the provisions of this Act, shall proceed in conformity with such laws, and nothing herein shall in any way affect any right of any State or of the Federal Government or of any landowner, appropriator, or user of water in, to, or from any interstate stream or the waters thereof: *Provided,* That the right to the use of water acquired under the provisions of this Act shall be appurtenant to the land irrigated, and beneficial use shall be the basis, the measure, and the limit of the right.

Sec. 9. That it is hereby declared to be the duty of the Secretary of the Interior in carrying out the provisions of this Act, so far as the same may be practicable and subject to the existence of feasible irrigation projects, to expend the major portion of the funds arising from the sale of public lands within each State and Territory hereinbefore named for the benefit of arid and semiarid lands within the limits of such State or Territory: *Provided,* That the Secretary may temporarily use such portion of said funds for the benefit of arid or semiarid lands in any particular State or Territory hereinbefore named as he may deem advisable, but when so used the excess shall be restored to the fund as soon as practicable, to the end that ultimately, and in any event, within each ten-year period after the passage of this Act, the expenditures for the benefit of the said States and Territories shall be equalized according to the proportions and subject to the conditions as to practicability and feasibility aforesaid.

Sec. 10. That the Secretary of the Interior is hereby authorized to perform any and all acts and to make such rules and regulations as may be necessary and proper for the purpose of carrying the provisions of this Act into full force and effect.

APPENDIX F

BIBLIOGRAPHY

General and Historical

Baldwin, J., The Conquest of the Old Northwest. American Book Co., New York. 50 cents.

Bandelier, Adolph F., The Delight Makers. Dodd, Mead & Co., New York. $1.25.

Brooks, N., First Across the Continent. Charles Scribner's Sons, New York. $1.50, net.

Casson, Herbert N., The Romance of Steel in America. A. S. Barnes & Co., New York. $2.50.

Chandler, Julian A., and O. P. Chitwood, Makers of American History. Silver, Burdette & Co., New York. 60 cents.

Cordley, R., Pioneer Days in Kansas. Pilgrim Press, Boston. $1.00, net.

Drake, Samuel A., The Making of the Great West. Charles Scribner's Sons, New York. $1.50.

Earle, Alice M., Home Life in Colonial Days. The Macmillan Co., New York. $2.50.

Fernow, B. E., Economics of Forestry. Thomas Y. Crowell & Co., New York. $1.50.

Gregg, David, Makers of the American Republic. E. B. Treat & Co., New York. $2.00.

Hulbert, A. B., The Ohio River; A Course of Empire. G. P. Putnam's Sons, New York. $3.50.

Inman, Henry, The Old Santa Fé Trail. The Macmillan Co., New York. $2.50.

Jenks, Tudor, When America Was New. Thomas Y. Crowell & Co., New York. $1.25.

Lummis, Charles F., Spanish Pioneers. A. C. McClurg & Co., Chicago, Ill. $1.50.

McMurray, Charles, Pioneers of the Rocky Mountains and Northwest. The Macmillan Co., New York. 40 cents, net.

Moore, Charles, The Northwest Under Three Flags. Harper & Brothers, New York. $2.50.

Mowry, W. A., The Territorial Growth of the United States. Silver, Burdette & Co., New York. $1.50.

Newell, Fred H., Irrigation in the United States. Thomas Y. Crowell & Co., New York. $2.00.

Paine, Ralph D., The Greater America. Outing Publishing Co., Deposit, N. Y. $1.50, net.

Parkman, F., The California and Oregon Trail. Thomas Y. Crowell & Co., New York. 50 cents.

Prince, Leon C., A Bird's-Eye View of American History. Charles Scribner's Sons, New York. $1.25.

Roosevelt, Theodore, Winning of the West. 4 vols. G. P. Putnam's Sons, New York. $10.00.

Semple, Ellen C., American History and Its Geographic Conditions. Houghton, Mifflin & Co., Boston. $3.00, net.

Smythe, William E., The Conquest of Arid America. The Macmillan Co., New York. $1.50.

Sparhawk, F. C., A Chronicle of Conquest. Lothrop, Lee & Sheppard, Boston. $1.00.

Standard History on Period 1840-1860.

Strong, Josiah, Our Country. Baker & Taylor Co., New York. 60 cents.

Van Dyke, John C., The Desert. Charles Scribner's Sons, New York. $1.25.

White, Stewart E., The Blazed Trail. McClure, Phillips & Co., New York. $1.50.

White, Stewart E., The Westerners. McClure, Phillips & Co., New York. $1.50.

American Commonwealth Series. Houghton, Mifflin & Co., Boston. Each $1.25 and $1.10: Virginia, by J. E. Cook; Oregon, by F. H. Hodder; California, by Josiah Royce; Ohio, by Rufus King; Michigan, by T. W. Cooley; Kansas, by L. W. Spring; Indiana, by J. P. Dunn, Jr.

Missions

Adams, Ephraim, The Iowa Band. Pilgrim Press, Boston. $1.00.

Clark, Joseph B., Leavening the Nation. Baker & Taylor Co., New York. $1.25, net.

Connor, Ralph, The Sky Pilot. Fleming H. Revell Co., New York. $1.25.

Connor, Ralph, Black Rock. Fleming H. Revell Co., New York. $1.25.

Connor, Ralph, The Prospector. Fleming H. Revell Co., New York. $1.50.

Connor, Ralph, The Doctor. Fleming H. Revell Co., New York. $1.50.

Craighead, J. G., A Story of Marcus Whitman. Presbyterian Board of Publication, Philadelphia. $1.00.

Crowell, Katherine R., The Call of the Waters. Fleming H. Revell Co., New York. 50 cents.

Doyle, Sherman H., Presbyterian Home Missions. Presbyterian Board of Home Missions, New York. 75 cents.

Eggleston, Edward, The Circuit Rider and Hoosier Schoolmaster. E. P. Judd, New Haven, Conn. $1.25.

Hines, H. K., Missionary History of the Pacific Northwest. H. K. Hines, Portland, Ore.

McAfee, Joseph E., Missions Striking Home. Fleming H. Revell Co., New York. 75 cents.

McLanahan, Samuel, et al., Home Mission Heroes. Presbyterian Board Home Missions, New York. 35 cents.

Morris, S. E., At Our Own Door. Fleming H. Revell Co., New York. $1.00, net.

Mowry, W. A., Marcus Whitman. Silver, Burdette & Co., New York. $1.50.

Nixon, O. W., How Marcus Whitman Saved Oregon. Star Publishing Co., Chicago, Ill. $1.50.

Phillips, Alexander L., The Call of the Homeland. Presbyterian Board of Publication, Richmond, Va. 50 cents.

Platt, Ward, Methodism and the Republic. Board of Home Missions and Church Extension, M. E. Church, Philadelphia. 50 cents.

Puddefoot, W. G., The Minute Man on the Frontier. T. Y. Crowell & Co., New York. $1.25.

Shelton, Don O., Heroes of the Cross in America. Young People's Missionary Movement, New York. 50 cents.

Sherwood, James M., Memoirs of David Brainerd. Funk & Wagnalls Co., New York. $1.50.

Smith, Justin, History of the Baptists West of the Mississippi River. American Baptist Publication Society, Philadelphia. 50 cents.

Stewart, Robert L., Sheldon Jackson. Fleming H. Revell Co., New York. $2.00.

Talbot, Ethelbert, My People of the Plains. Harper & Bros., New York. $1.65, net.

Tomlinson, Everett T., The Fruit of the Desert. The Griffith & Rowland Press, Philadelphia. $1.25.

Tompson, C. Lemuel, The Presbyterian. Baker & Taylor Co., New York. $1.00, net.

Tuttle, Daniel S., Reminiscences of a Missionary Bishop. Thomas Whittaker, New York. $2.00, net.

Whipple, Henry B., Lights and Shadows of a Long Episcopate. The Macmillan Co., New York. $2.50, net.

White, Greenough, An Apostle of the Western Church, Bishop Kemper. Thomas Whittaker, New York. $1.50, net.

Young, Egerton R., An Apostle of the North. Fleming H. Revell Co., New York. $1.25.

American Indians

Eells, Myra, Ten Years' Mission Work Among Indians at Skokomish. Pilgrim Press, Boston. $1.25.

Finley, James B., Life Among the Indians. Methodist Book Concern, New York. 90 cents.

Humphrey, Seth K., The Indian Dispossessed. Little, Brown & Co., Boston. $1.50.

Jackson, Helen H., A Century of Dishonor. Little, Brown & Co., Boston. $1.50.

Johnston, Julia H., Indian and Spanish Neighbors. Fleming H. Revell Co., New York. 50 cents.

McBeth, Kate C., The Nez Perces Indians Since Lewis and Clark. Fleming H. Revell Co., New York. $1.50, net.

Pond, Samuel M., Two Volunteer Missionaries Among the Dakotas. Pilgrim Press, Boston. $1.25.

Sparhawk, Francis C., Onoqua. Lothrop, Lee & Sheppard, Boston. $1.00.

Strong, James C., Wah-kee-nah and Her People. G. P. Putnam's Sons, New York. $1.25.

Wood, Norman B., Lives of Famous Indian Chiefs. American Indian Historical Publishing Co., Aurora, Ill. $2.50.

Young, Egerton R., Algonquin Indian Tales. Fleming H. Revell Co., New York. $1.25.

Young, Egerton R., Child of the Forest. Fleming H. Revell Co., New York. $1.25.

Young, Egerton R., On the Indian Trail. Fleming H. Revell Co., New York. $1.00.

Magazine References

Irrigation, Dry Farming, Forestry, and Related Subjects

Anderson. "Irrigation in Southwestern United States and Mexico." Out West, August, '06.

Barnes, "Gifford Pinchot, Forester." McClure's Magazine, July, '08.

Beacom, "Irrigation in the United States: Its Geographical and Economic Results." Geographical Journal, April, '07.

Blackwelder, "A Country That Has Used Up Its Trees." Outlook, March 24, '06.

Blanchard, "A Stupendous International Irrigation Project." Leslie's Weekly, March 14, '07.

Casson, "The New American Farmer." Review of Reviews, May, '08.

Cope, "Making Gardens Out of Lava-dust." World To-Day, June, '06.

Cowan, "Dry Farming the Hope of the West." Century Magazine, July, '06.

Deming, "Irrigation Problems in Wyoming." Independent, May 9, '07.

Deming, "Dry Farming; What It Is." Independent, April 18, '07.

Donahue, "Farming Without Water." World To-Day, August, '06.

Dunn, "One Tree to Save a State's Lumber Supply." Technical World Magazine, August, '08.

Edmonds, "A National Inventory." Review of Reviews, May, '08.

Fernow, "Saving the Waste of Forests." Country Life in America, August, '07.

Fielde, "Lumbering in Washington." Independent, November 7, '07.

Forbes-Lindsay, "Spending a Billion and a Half Dollars to Make a Desert Bloom." Harper's Weekly, February 2, '07.

Geiser, "Results of Forestry in Germany." World's Work, March, '07.

Hays, "The American Farmer Feeding the World." World's Work, August, '08.

Hough, "The Slaughter of the Trees." Everybody's Magazine, May, '08.

Jenkins, "Reclaiming Arid Lands Near Denver." National Magazine, July, '08.

Kirkbride, "One-Acre Ranch." Century Magazine, March, '08.

Kirkwood, "The Romantic Story of a Scientist." World's Work, April, '08.

Mitchell, "Checking the Waste of Our National Resources." Review of Reviews, May, '08.

Nelson, "The Lumber Industry of America." Review of Reviews, November, '07.

Page, "The Rediscovery of Our Greatest Wealth." World's Work, May, '08.

Pinchot, "The Conservation of National Resources." Outlook, October 12, '07.

Quick, "Farming Without Water." World's Work, August, '06.

Roosevelt, "Forest and Reclamation Service of the United States." National Geographic Magazine, November, '06.

Sterling, "Reforestation in Southern California." Out West, July, '07.

Taylor, "Economic Problems in Agriculture by Irrigation." Journal of Political Economy, April, '07.

Vanderhoof, "Irrigating an Empire." World To-Day, August, '08.

Van Dyke, "In the Big Woods of Oregon." Outing Magazine, February, '06.

Will, "Forestry: Planting Trees for Profit." World's Work, November, '07.

Wright, "The Government as a Home Maker." World To-Day, February, '06.

Appendix F

Railways and Waterways

Baker, "Destiny and the Western Railroad." Century Magazine, April, '08.

Carr, "The New Northwest and the Railways." Outlook, August 24, '07.

Cochrane, "Why Railroads Are Busy." Moody's Magazine, January, '07.

Larkin, "A Thousand Men Against a River." World's Work, March, '07.

Mathews, "The Future of Our Navigable Waters." Atlantic Monthly, December, '07.

Mathews, "The New Mississippi." Everybody's Magazine, April, '08.

McGee, "Our Dawning Waterway Era." World's Work, April, '08.

McGee, "Our Inland Waterways." Popular Science Monthly, April, '08.

Prosser, "Railways Divide a New Kingdom." Technical World Magazine, August, '08.

Tait, "Taming the Mississippi." World To-Day, March, '07.

Willey, "A War Against a River." Wide World Magazine, August, '08.

The Northwest

Borah, "The Citizenship of Idaho." Pacific Monthly, February, '08.

Carr, "The Great Northwest." Outlook, June 22, '07.

Chapple, "Triumphs of the Canadian West." National Geographic Magazine, August, '07.

Cushman, "The Northwest Gateway of Our Commerce." The Outing Magazine, February, '08.

Elford, "Oregon: An Inland Empire." Overland Monthly, June, '05.

Elrod, "Resources of Montana and Their Development." Science, May 20, '04.

Gooding, "The Promise of Idaho." Pacific Monthly, February, '08.

Hunter, "Idaho." Pacific Monthly, February, '08.

Lloyd, "Where Rolls the Oregon." Outing Magazine, February, '06.

Lockley, "Westward Ho to Idaho." Pacific Monthly, February, '08.

Mills, "Economic Struggle in Colorado." Arena, February, March, May, October, '06.

Moorehead, "Crossing the Great Divide by Electricity." World's Work, April, '08.

Northrop, "The Great Northwest." World To-Day, January, '06.

Oberholtzer, "Opening of the Great Northwest." Century Magazine, March, '07.

Reed, "The Empire of the Northern Prairies." World To-Day, February, '08.

Thomas, "Our Own Northwest." Success Magazine, October and November, '07.

Van Dyke, "Big Woods of Oregon." Outing Magazine, February, '06.

Willey, "The Folk of the Puget Sound Country." Outing Magazine, February, '06.

Wolf, "The Inland Empire." Pacific Monthly, May, '07.

The Mormons

Davis, "Practical Results of Mormonism." Missionary Review of the World, March, '07.

Horwill, "Investigation of Mormon Church." Albany Review, June, '07.

Kinney, "Present Situation Among the Mormons." Missionary Review of the World, August, '06.

The Southwest

Bessey, "Vegetation of Texas." Science, April 19, '07.

Brownell, "Oklahoma: The Fight for Statehood." Appleton's Magazine, April, '07.

Cunniff, "Texas and the Texans." World's Work, March, '06.

Cunniff, "The New State of Oklahoma." World's Work, June, '06.

Currie, "The Transformation of the Southwest through the Legal Abolition of Gambling." Century Magazine, April, '08.

Dinwiddie, "Oklahoma: To-Day and To-Morrow." Appleton's Magazine, April, '07.

"Growth of Southwest Texas." Review of Reviews, February, '06.

Harvey, "The Southwest's Evolution." Metropolitan Magazine, August, '08.

Harvey, "The Great Southwest." Munsey's Magazine, March, '05.

Hough, "The Rise of the State of Oklahoma." Appleton's Magazine, April, '07.

Hough: "Oklahoma: the Coming of the White Man." Appleton's Magazine, April, '07.

Matson, "The Awakening of Nevada." Review of Reviews, July, '06.

McGuire, "Big Oklahoma." National Geographic Magazine, February, '06.

Ogden, "The Newest Land of Promise." Everybody's Magazine, November, '07.

Ogden, "Farming in the Southwest." Everybody's Magazine, November, '07.

Willey, "The Southwestern Oil Fields." Moody's Magazine, January, '07.

The West Between and Beyond

Blanchard, "The Quickening of Nevada." Pacific Monthly, May, '07.

Dutton, "Our Strategic Position on the Pacific." Pacific Monthly, November, '07.

McAdie, "Climate of the Pacific Coast." Outing Magazine, February, '06.

Reinhart, "Seizing the Desert's Last Stronghold." World's Work, April, '08.

The American Indians

Brown, "The Indians and Oklahoma." Outlook, January 19, '07.

Forbes-Lindsay, "Shaping the Future of the Indians." World To-Day, March, '07.

Kennan, "Lands of Indians and Fair Play." Outlook, February 27, '04.

Leupp, "Gospel of Work for Indians." Nation, October 6, '04.

Oskison, "Making an Individual of the Indian." Everybody's Magazine, June, '07.

Oskison, "Remaining Causes of Indian Discontent." North American Review, March 1, '07.

Sparhawk, "The Indian's Yoke." North American Review, January, '06.

Willey, "Our Other Race Problem." Metropolitan Magazine, October, '07.

Chinese, Japanese, and Some Other People

Brooks, "The Real Pacific Question." Harper's Weekly, October 12, '07.

Dodd, "The Hindus in the Northwest." World To-Day, November, '07.

Fulton, "Japanese Pupils in American Schools." North American Review, December 21, '06.

Hart, "The Japanese in California." World's Work, March, '07.

Harwood, "Extinction of the Chinese in the United States." World's Work, December, '04.

Ichihashi, "Japanese Students in America." Outlook, October 12, '07.

Inglis, "Reasons for California's Attitude Toward Japanese." Harper's Weekly, January 19, '07.

Irwin, "The Japanese and the Pacific Coast." Collier's Weekly, September 28, '07; October 12, 19, 26, '07.

Irwin, "Chinese Slave Trade in California." Everybody's Magazine, July, '04.

Kawakami, "Naturalization of the Japanese." North American Review, June 21, '07.

Kawakami, "The Japanese in California." Independent, November 29, '06.

Kessler, "An Evening in Chinatown." Overland Monthly, May, '07.

Lockley, "The Hindu Invasion." Pacific Monthly, May, '07.

Lusk, "The Real Yellow Peril." North American Review, November, '07.

Maitland, "Chinese in California and South Africa." Contemporary Review, December, '05.

Miller, "The Ruinous Cost of Chinese Exclusion." North American Review, November, '07.

Nickerson, "Chinese Treaties and Legislation of the United States and Their Enforcement." North American Review, September, '05.

Scheffauer, "The Old Chinese Quarter, San Francisco." Macmillan's Magazine, July, '07.

Thomson, "Japanese in San Francisco." World To-Day, December, '06.

Wherry, "Hindu Immigrants in America." Missionary Review of the World, December, '07.

Miscellaneous

"American Trade Around the World." World's Work, August, '08.

Brock, "The Americanism of the Last West." Outing Magazine, February, '06.

Cameron, "Wheat the Wizard of the North." Atlantic Monthly, December, '07.

Dickey, "The Modern Pioneer." World To-Day, February, '08.

Harger, "Revival in Western Land Values." Review of Reviews, January, '07.

Harvey, "A School for American Business Men." Appleton's Magazine, February, '08.

Harvey, "Epics of the West's Expansion." North American Review, July 5, '07.

McCandless, "Hawaii, the Cross-roads of the Pacific." World's Work, March, '07.

Moody, "The Real Cowboy." Outdoor Life, February, '07.

Rowe, "Our Trade Relations with South America." North American Review, March 1, '07.

Sherman, "Followers of the Bunch Grass Hunter." Outing Magazine, February, '06.

Straus, "Our Era of Commercial Greatness." World's Work, August, '08.

True, "The Coming of Law to the Frontier." Outing Magazine, February, '08.

Watson, "Copper Wealth in a Remarkable New Camp." Leslie's Weekly, March 14, '07.

Willey, "America in the Orient." Putnam's Magazine, July, '08.

Wright, "Westward to the Far East." Pacific Monthly, May, '07.

A great number of issues of several board periodicals and publications, for the last three years, also their leaflets, are of special value.

The denominational reports will repay reading.

INDEX

INDEX

A

Abraham's westward call, 248
Absorption of the American Indian, 198
Africa and the West as mission fields, 105
Agricultural college a world asset, 82
Agriculture the basis of civilization, 42
"Aim-day-co," 202
Alfalfa, an acclimated, 83
Altruistic spirit, the, 207
American Board in Oregon, 20
American History and Its Geographic Conditions quoted, 3
American Revolution, the, 6
Anglo-Saxon blood, 4, 32; the modern Anglo-Saxon, 184
Appalachian Mountains, 6-8
Arctic Circle and wheat, 88
Arctic Ocean, 6
Area of the United States, 4
"Argonauts of '49," the, 25
Arid West, our, 46
Aridity a blessing, 43, 46
Arizona, 153, 159-163; as a health resort, 161; bullfights in, 157; the Roosevelt Reservoir, 160
Armada, the Spanish, 14
Artesian wells, 151; in Pecos Valley, 164
Asia, a source of improved products, 82, 83; its missionary aspect from the West, 111, 145-147, 174-177, 209-215, 249
Atlantic Ocean and the colonies, 9

B

Bacon as fuel, 12
Balboa, 14
Barnes's "Gifford Pinchot, Forester" referred to, 61.
"Big Pasture," Oklahoma, 166
Billings, Montana, 81
Blanchard, C. J., referred to, 53, 258
Boston and the early fur trade, 16
Boundary line, the northern, 21, 22
Brainerd, David, 188
Buddhism in San Francisco, 146
Burbank, Luther, referred to, 82
Butte copper mines, 84

C

California, discovery of gold in, 24; early settlers in, 23; present conditions in, 144; Spain in, 14
California Trail, 25
Canada, annexation and reciprocity, 89

284 Index

Canadian Northwest, Americans in the, 88; railroads, 89
Canyons, 48
Cape Prince of Wales, 13
Capen, S. B., quoted, 233
Caravans cross the continent, 21, 22
Carson Basin, Nevada, 129, 142
Cascade Mountains, 44
Cattle-ranges and irrigation, 56
Center of power, 4
Central City, Colorado, 121
Chili, 173
China, awakening, 90; early fur trade with, 15; possible productiveness, 4
Chinese, in America, 212; characteristics and ill-treatment of, 213; home missions among, 215
Churches, the call to the, 66, 225–240
Civil War reminiscences, 89
Civilizations contrasted, two, 207
Climate of the U. S., 3; causes of, 4
Coast Range, the, 118
Colorado, altitude of, 117; climate, gold mining, products, resources, 119; irrigated land, 119; public-spirited men, 120; railways, 120; religious interests in, 121, 122
Colorado River, the, 48
Colorado Springs, 120
Columbia River named by Captain Gray, 16
Columbia River pass, 78, 79
Congress, land grants by, 9

Connecticut's missionary work, 33
Conquest of Arid America, The, referred to, 41, 259
Consecration, the highest, 246
Cook, Captain, 13, 15, 17
Cook, Rev. Charles, referred to, 203
Coöperative spirit, a, 55
Copper in Montana, 84
Corner lots secured for churches, 103
Corpus Christi, Texas, market-gardening in, 169
Cotton, in Oklahoma, 167; in Texas, 173
Council, Idaho, its mission work, 96
Crops, irrigation insures a series of, 47; order of, in dry farming, 63, 64
Crossing the continent, Lee and Whitman, 21, 22

D

Dakotas, climate of the, 4; the people, 87
Dawes act of 1887, 198
Deception Bay, 16
Deming, in *The Independent*, referred to, 64
Democracy, a backwoods, 7
Denver, 120
Desert, hardships of, 13, 28, 31; holiday experiences in, 30; transformation of, 41; underground lakes in, 51
Destruction of our forests, 60
Development, begins westward, 10; varied in western states, 118

Ditching, prehistoric models in, 48
Doors opened by cotton and wheat, 173
Doyle, Dr. S. H., quoted on Indian affairs, 190-197
Dry farming, 63-65, 82

E

Edwards, Jonathan, referred to, 188
Efforts of the churches, 103
El Paso, Texas, 170, 207
Electricity, in desert work, 51; in developing towns, 57
Eliot, John, referred to, 188
Ely, Nevada, 140
Engineering feats in western work, 52
England's Pacific possessions, 4
English pioneer, the, 3
Enlightenment needed, concerning home missions, 227, 229; literature fragmentary, 231; loss from lack of knowledge, 235
Enthroning the Christ, 237
Everybody's Magazine referred to, 60
Exemplary church, an, 241
Explorations, European, in North America, 5; on the Pacific coast, 13
Extension of the United States, 9

F

"Five Civilized Tribes" of Oklahoma, 199
Flag carried around the globe, our, 16
Foreign countries represented in the Dakotas, 99-101
Forest, the function of the, 59
Forestry department, our, 61
Fort Hall, 23
Foster, at Council, Idaho, 96; his wife "Minnie," 97, 98
Fremont, John C., 24
French, nation, 18; trader, 8
"From passage to peltries," 5
Frontier in the making, our, 3
Frontier preachers, 91-94
Fruit grown in irrigated regions, 116
Fur trade, and exploration, 6; with China, 15, 16

G

Gadsden Purchase, 13
Gallatin Valley, Montana, 81
Galveston, Texas, 170, 174
Gambling being driven out of the Southwest, 157
Gateway of the Upper Rio Grande, 11
Generosity of converted heathen, 232
Gentile influence in Utah, 136
Geography, its bearing on early development of United States, 3
Giant Northwest, the, 75-114
Gila Trail, 12
Goal, the destined, 223

God, nature an expression of, 34
Gold in California, discovery of, 24
Golden spike driven, 26
Goldfield, Nevada, 140
Governmental action in irrigation development, 49, 50
Gray, Captain, discovers and names Columbia River, 16
"Great American Desert," the, 128; physical features, 129
"Great Interior Basin," our, 128-130
Great Lakes, the, 6
Greeley Colony, 120
Gulf, breezes from, 4

H

Harwood, Dr. Thomas, of Albuquerque, 209
Hawaii, 89; Japanese in, 210, 211; location of, 5
Heroic leaders, 226
Hill, Mr. James J., quoted, 76
Holland in the New World, 14
Home and foreign heathen, 230, 237
Home mission fields, 66
Home missionary heroes, 226; the home missionary, 35
Homes, motive in western emigration, 43, 50; result from irrigation, 57; the object in governmental action, 62, 63
Homesteaders in the Dakotas, 101
Hudson's Bay Company, 20
Hudson Valley, 7
Humid and arid regions contrasted agriculturally, 56; our humid sections, 45
Humphrey, S. K., quoted, 182

I

Idaho, 77, 81; conditions in, 138; mining town, 96; Mormons, 138; pastor's experience, 66; physical features, 118; Twin Falls church, 138; unreached in, 105
Ignorance a peril, 227
Immigration, Napoleonic wars and, 10
Imperial Valley, Arizona, 129, 155
Independence, Missouri, 11
India, the attitude of, 90
Indian affairs, Dr. S. H. Doyle quoted on, 190-197
Indian and Spanish Neighbors quoted, 197, 201
Indian and the white man, the, 185
Indians, American, 181-207; missions to, 188, 189, 200-207; policy of government toward, 18, 186, 192-199; present population, 190, 191
Indian Territory, the, 11; Indians of, 199
Individual man a chief factor in progress, 247
Intensive farming, 47, 81
Internal development, 41
Irrigated arid regions and fruit growing, 116

Index

Irrigation, 40–59, 116, 123, 129, 130, 164, 225; by governmental action, 49–57; provision for fund, 50, 259–264

J

James, G. W., quoted, 182
Japan, 90; as a competitor, 4
Japanese, as immigrants, 209; colony in Texas, 175; occupations of, 211; statistics, 210
Jefferson's tactful plea to congress, 18
Jews in the Southwest, 176
Johnston, Julia H., quoted, 197, 201
Journeys of pioneer times, 27
Juarez, Mexico, 207

K

Kansas, conformation of, 117
Kansas City a portal, 117
Key to interpret history, 186
Kit Carson's ride, 12
Kynett, Dr. A. J., xi

L

Lake Nicaragua, 14
"Last man," the, 197, 199
Lee, Rev. Jason, 19, 85; conducts colony to Oregon, 21; missionary and patriotic services, 19–21
Lewis and Clark, 11, 18, 19
Local church methods, 240
"Lone Star" flag, the, 24
Los Angeles, 12

Louisiana Purchase, the, 9, 17
Lumber, camps, 92; shipments, 80; welcome of mission work, 92, 93

M

Macaroni wheat grown in the Northwest, 83
Macedonian call, a new, 179
Marshall, James W., 24
Massacre, Whitman's, 22
McAfee, James E., quoted, 222
Mexican government, the, 24
Mexicans, 207; mission schools for, 208
Mexico and Spain, 14
Millennium, a hastened, 245
Mines and mining, 25, 84, 94–96, 118, 130, 139, 140; church conditions in mining camps and towns, 94–96
Minidoka government irrigation project, the, 66–68
Minnesota's boundary line, 44; her people, 88
Minute Man on the Frontier quoted, 35
Mission, call to young people, 247, 248; responsibility of the Churches, 111, 146, 147, 177, 182, 207, 222–249; prayer-meetings, 240; study classes, 241, 242; training of the Sunday-school, 242
Missionaries in home fields, courage and optimism, 108, 109; perils and sacrifices, 22, 23, 32–35, 67, 97, 98, 107, 108, 122, 135, 188, 244–247

Missions and missionary conditions, among Chinese, 212–215; among Indians, 200–207; among Japanese, 209 – 212; among Mexicans, 207–209; in the Northwest, 89–108; in the "West Between," 118–146; in the Southwest, 155–177
Mississippi River, 17
Missouri, productive soil, 12; River, 18, 47
Mohawk Valley, 7
Monroe Doctrine, 13
Montana, 77, 81; climate, 4; people, 87; railways, 84; unreached population, 105
Mormon, ambitions, 134; convert's story, 137; influence of missionary schools, 133; most difficult field, 135; outlook and results, 136–139
Mormons, in Idaho, 138; in Utah, 131; irrigation by the Mormons, 129

N

Napoleonic wars and immigration, 10
National Geographic Magazine referred to, 53
Nature and God, workers with, 184
Nebraska's conformation, 117
Needs of the Northwest, 92
Nevada, area, population, possibilities, 130; churches, 140; farmers, 116; irrigation, 129, 142; missionary's statement, 141; physical conditions, 139; railroads, 142; State University, 140
New England Christian enterprise, 33
New Mexico, 153, 155; conditions in, 163; Pecos Valley section, 163; population, 163, 164; resources, 164
New settlement conditions, 157, 225
New Southwest, the, 151–180; climate, extent, people, 153; growth, 154; religious foundations, 155
Nez Percés Indians at St. Louis, 19, 85
Nile Valley cited, 46
Noble work of young men, 53
North Dakota, 77, 81, 99, 100
Northwest, along the Pacific, 14–23; the Canadian, 88; the Early, 7; the Giant, 75–114; crucial missionary conditions, 99; problems, 90
Northwest passage, search for a, 5, 14, 15

O

Obedience measures power, 238
Obstruction reveals swift current, 183
Ocean liners, Pacific, 84
Ogden, Utah, 26
Oklahoma, 153; church needs, 167, 168, 245; development of and opportunities in, 165, 166; population, products, progress, 16–167

Index

Oregon, American Board in, 20; claim of United States, 16-23; comparative size, 77; emigration to, 12; Lee and Whitman's colonies, 21, 22; people of, 85; provisional government in,22; United States claim upon, 19; unreached in, 105
Oregon Trail, 12
Orient, the, and San Francisco, 145; our commerce with the East and mission work, 91
Orientward trend in commerce and missions, 5, 76, 78-85, 89-91, 111, 144-147, 171-177, 209-215, 249

P

Pacific Northwest, the, 14-23
Pacific Ocean, territory bordering on the, 4, 5, 14
Pacific winds and the Rockies, 4
Paine, *The Greater America*, quoted, 76, 102
Panama Canal, 14, 170, 171
Panhandle of Texas, 169
Panic times, thoughtful contributions in, 234
"Pathfinder, the," 24
Paul's call westward, 248
Passion for missions, a, 233
Pecos Valley, New Mexico, 164
People of the Northwest, the, 85, 86
Philippines, the, 89
Pima church in Sacaton, 203
Pinchot, Gifford, 61

Pioneer, hardships, 27-31, 65; placing of successors under obligation, 31; results to Indian life, 187, 188; spirit, 8, 13
Polygamy in Utah, 131, 132
Population, as affected by irrigation, 56; by railways, 26; table showing recent increase by states, 256
Portland, Oregon, 79, 85
Porto Rico, 171
Possible results of irrigation, 49
Powell quoted, 116
Power from irrigation plants, 51
Preachers, on the frontier, 91, 104, 107-109; wives of, 108, 246
Prehistoric models in ditching, 48
Problems, Asiatic immigration, 90; of irrigation works, 53; of the Northwest, 89
Progress, the march of, 188
Prohibition in North Dakota, 87
Projects in irrigation, 258
Protestantism, in Colorado, 121; in the Southwest, 155
Public lands, our, 45
Puddefoot, W. G., quoted, 35, 152
Puget Sound, 21, 78; contiguous resources, 80; freight facilities, 85

Q

Qualities born of hardships, 13

R

Railroads, dominate the West, 117, 223, 224; electric traction, 84; extension in the Northwest, 83; first transcontinental, 9; the lead in trackage, 170; in Texas, 170; in the Great Basin, 130
Rainless sections in the United States, 45
Reclaimed arid sections, 48, 56
Religious aspect in new towns, 58, 106
Reno, Nevada, the State University at, 140
Reserves, our forest, 61
Responsibility, our, 111, 243–249
Rhode Island's population and that of irrigated districts compared, 58
Rice culture in Texas, 175
Ridley, Bishop, quoted, 202
Rio Grande, a sugar-cane region, 169
Riverside, California, 57
Rocky Mountains, 11, 44, 102, 103, 117
Roosevelt Reservoir, 160
Roosevelt, Theodore, trained on a western ranch, 62; tribute to Indian missionaries, 205
Russia as a trade competitor of the United States, 4

S

Sacramento Valley, 23, 25
Saloons becoming unpopular in Arizona, 157
Salt Lake City, 129, 136
San Diego, 12, 15
San Francisco, 24; a gateway to the Orient, 117; importance of, 144; Japanese aid when needed, 212; longer and more mountainous route for overland freight, 78, 79; mission work in, 145, 146
Santa Fé, old buildings in, 163
Santa Fé Trail, 12
Scandinavians, 88
Schafer, Joseph, xi; referred to, 26
Seed selection, results of, 82, 83
Self-investment, 236, 239, 247
Selfishness, 232; to be overcome in the home Church, 232
Semiarid belt, 65
Semple, Ellen Churchill, x; quoted, 3
Shelton, Don O., quoted, 222
Sierra range of mountains, 44, 118
Small farms under the irrigation system, 56
Smalley quoted, 76
Smoot case, the, 136
Smythe, William E., xi; quoted, 40, 116; referred to, 41
Social order, an ideal, 55
Soil in the arid West, 46
Soul rest, 240
South America, 171, 172
South Dakota, 77, 81; railroads and incoming settlers, 100–103; superin-

Index 291

tendent's district, 104; the Indians of, 204
Southwest, the, 152; health-seekers in, 161; pastoral care desired, 162; sanitariums needed, 163; the outlook, 171
Spain in the New World, 14, 16; present attitude, 89
Spanish, Armada, 14; Trail, 12
Spokane, country, 103; River, 84
Standard of missionary devotion for young people, 248
Statistics, agriculture, people engaged in, in 1900, 42; American farmers going to Canadian Northwest, 88; California, population in 1870, 25; Chinese population, 212; Colorado products, 119, 120; educational appropriation for Indians, 198; farms, in 1900, 42; forest reserves, area, 60, 61; Gadsden Purchase, price paid, 13; Indians, main classes, 190, 191; irrigation projects, area and cost, 49, 258; Japanese population, 210; Louisiana Purchase, churches, 228; Oklahoma towns and cities, 166; Oregon Trail, length of, 12; Northwest, population in 1870 and 1880, 26; railroad new mileage, in Nevada, in 1907, 140; Southwest, population, 153; states, area and population, 256; territory added to United States, area and population, 255; Texas measurements, 152, 169, 170; United States, area, 4, 256; unreached populations in Oregon and Washington, 106, 107; vacant and reserved areas, 257
St. Louis, Nez Percés in, 19
Strong, Josiah, quoted, 2, 152
Sunday-school missionary training and work, 242
Supplies furnished by Woman's Home Missionary organizations, 108
Sutter, Captain John, 23

T

Table-land, extent of dry, 47
Taming the desert, 44
Taylor, Bishop William, 25
Teutons, the, 88
Texas, 152–154; advancement in, 168; crops, land, settlers in, 169
Tomlinson, Everett T., quoted, 92
Towns springing up in irrigated sections, 54, 56
Trails, historic, 11, 12
Transcontinental railway, the first, 26
Truckee-Carson irrigation scheme, 129, 140
Turner quoted, 2
Twin Falls, Idaho, the church at, 138

U

Underground lakes in the desert, 51
United States, course of discovery and settlement, 5-26; growth in territory, 9, 13, 17, 24, 255; internal development, 223, 224; well located for world influence, 3, 223
Urgent missionary needs, 225, 226
Utah, Mormonism, 131-138; physical features, population problems, 118

V

Vacant and reserved areas in western public land, 257
Vancouver, Captain, 17

W

Walla Walla River, 20
Washington, 77; conditions in, 106, 107
Water under the desert sand, 130
Watershed, a continental, 118
Wells, artesian, and irrigation, 51, 164
"West Between and Beyond," 115-149; dominated by railways, 117; great variety, 118; immense resources from soil and mines, 118-144
West, the, 2; gateway of the, 7; its importance, 5
Western expansion, our, 4
Western, frontier, our, 78; table-land, 44
Wheat, quality when grown toward Arctic Circle, 88; special hardy varieties, 83
Wheeler, Rev. O. C., 25
Whitman, Dr. Marcus, 20, 22, 85
Whole world for Christ, 228, 229
Willamette River, 19
Winning Christianity, a, 238
Wise beginnings made, 228
Woman, missionary, 201; suffrage states, 118
Woman's Home Missionary organizations aiding the work, 108
Working with nature and God transforms man, 184
World history, three stages of, 3
Wyoming, features of, 117, 118; irrigation law, 123; physical aspects and conditions in, 123-128; stock raising, 116

Z

Zulu Christians, and giving, 232

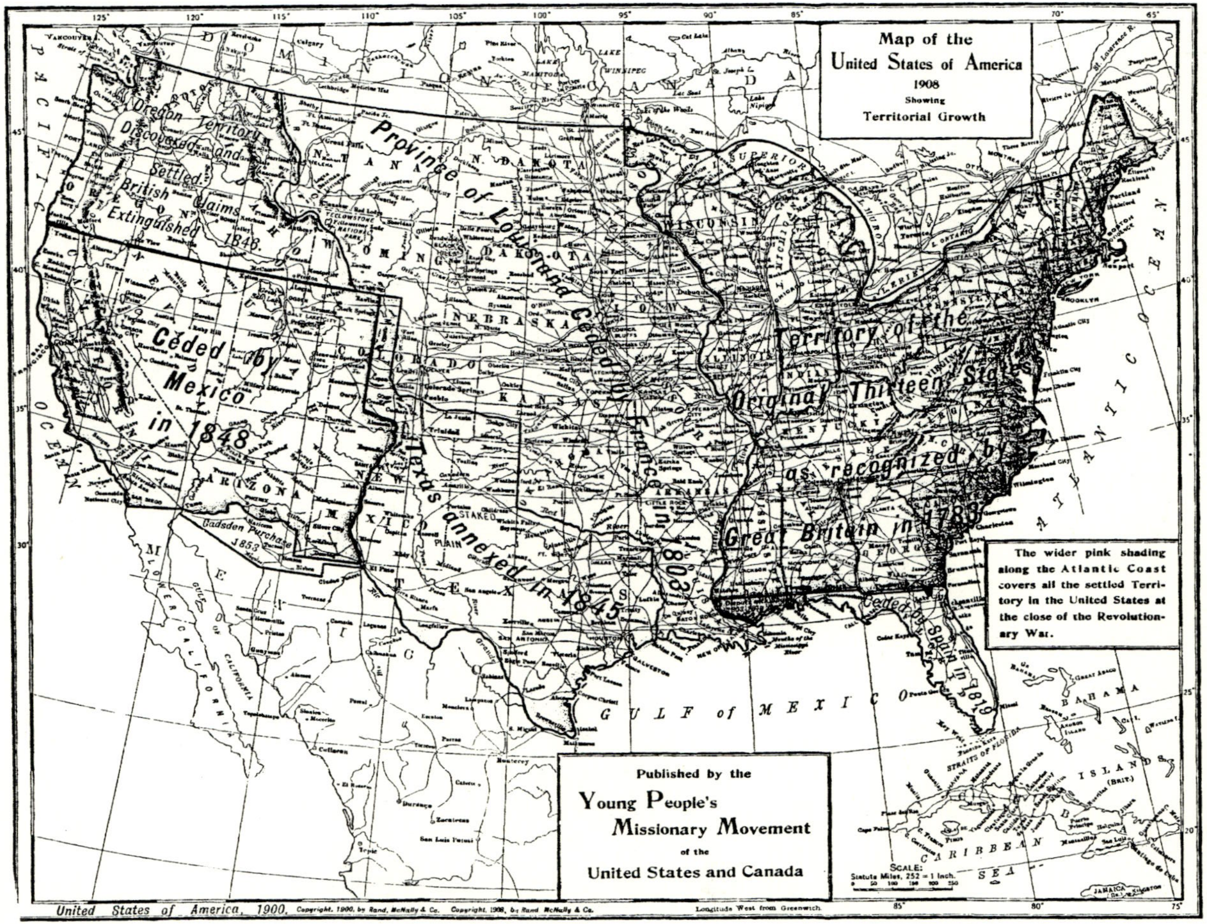
Map of the
United States of America
1908
Showing
Territorial Growth
Province of Louisiana Ceded by France in 1803
Oregon Territory Discovered and Settled. British Claims Extinguished 1846.
Ceded by Mexico in 1848
Texas annexed in 1845
Gadsden Purchase 1853
Territory of the Original Thirteen States as recognized by Great Britain in 1783
Ceded by Spain in 1819
The wider pink shading along the Atlantic Coast covers all the settled Territory in the United States at the close of the Revolutionary War.
Published by the
Young People's
Missionary Movement
of the
United States and Canada
PACIFIC OCEAN
ATLANTIC OCEAN
GULF of MEXICO
DOMINION OF CANADA
CARIBBEAN SEA
SCALE:
Statute Miles, 252 = 1 Inch.
United States of America, 1900. Copyright, 1900, by Rand, McNally & Co. Copyright, 1908, by Rand McNally & Co.
Longitude West from Greenwich